AREA·51 INTERNS

ZONED OUT

BY JAMES S. MURRAY AND CARSEN SMITH

PENGUIN WORKSHOP

To Mom, Dad, my family and my wife Melyssa—JSM
For Beth, Shirley, Art and Ernie—CS

PENGUIN WORKSHOP
An imprint of Penguin Random House LLC, New York

First published in the United States of America by Penguin Workshop,
an imprint of Penguin Random House LLC, New York, 2022

Insert illustrations by Patrick Spaziante

Insert HUD assets: NatalyaBurova/iStock/Getty Images, Nattapon Kongbunmee/iStock/Getty
Images, PlargueDoctor/iStock/Getty Images, SerGRAY/iStock/Getty Images, St_Aurora72/
iStock/Getty Images, Veronika Oliinyk/iStock/Getty Images

Visit us online at penguinrandomhouse.com.

Library of Congress Cataloging-in-Publication Data is available.

Printed in the United States of America

ISBN 9780593226148

10 9 8 7 6 5 4 3 2 1 CJKB

Design by Jay Emmanuel

CHAPTER ONE

Arrows sliced through the air above Viv's head. All around, echoes of horses' hooves pounded against the thick jungle floor of the terrarium.

But suddenly, it all went silent. Everyone else was gone, except for one lone knight riding a monstrous horse.

His metal breastplate clattered like a thousand pots and pans, and his banner flag whipped against the wind, tied inches below the glistening, sharp point of his lance.

He was the last one left. The final remnant of the chaos that had overtaken Area 51. Destruction lay all around as smoke, arrows, and shouting filled the air. The other knights who had burst from the wormhole had all been sent back through to their own dimension . . .

Leaving the most bloodthirsty of the bunch to finish the job.

Viv stood directly in his path, her arm cannon poised and ready to strike. She hoped her combat suit would protect her.

Come on! Come get me!

The knight let out a guttural scream that was nearly muffled by his massive, unruly beard. He kicked his horse in its haunches, accelerating even faster, thundering straight toward Viv.

Viv was ready. She planted her heels and wrapped her fingers around the trigger in her suit. The swirling darkness of the wormhole behind her shimmered in her peripheral vision as she stared down the knight's ever-approaching lance.

Almost there . . . just a bit closer.

When the horse was so near she could feel its spittle hit her cheek, that was when she made her move.

Here goes nothing.

Viv dodged quickly to the right, and the horse roared past. The knight, fury evident even beneath the beard, swiveled toward her. He brandished his lance and yanked hard on the reins, trying to pull his steed back from the approaching abyss. It looked like he might almost succeed, but Viv lined up her shot, fired off a blast. The knight hollered . . .

"Viv, stop drooling all over the place!"

Viv jolted out of the memory to see her best friend, Charlotte, staring down at her.

✳ ✳ ✳ ✳ ✳

Vivian Harlow stared out blankly across an ocean of paperwork, her wistful daydream cut short. Like the beating of the horse's hooves, her memories of last week still pounded through her head.

Seven days earlier, everything had felt so different. Viv and her friends had fought off a horde of escaped aliens that threatened to kidnap every human at Area 51 and hold them all prisoner in another galaxy. The four kids were treated like heroes, and Viv expected the internship that followed would feel the same. Thrilling. Exciting. A chance for them to show off their skills. And for a moment, when they'd all fought back the knights, it had been. But now that the wormholes were closed and the damage from the Roswellians had been cleaned up, business was back to normal at Area 51. The congratulations had worn off, and their parents had taken back their gadgets. Now she and her friends were just another group of low-level employees. The lowest level employees. They were just summer interns.

And like all interns throughout history, she and her friends had been assigned to a task that the staff had been putting off for years—filing away a decade's worth of old paperwork in the abandoned copy room. The task was simple: scan each page on the giant imaging machine, type the department name and date into the Central Brain—Area 51's hyper-advanced central intelligence system—and then shred the paper copies.

At this point, Viv's fingers were on autopilot. Exhaustion threatened to pull her eyelids closed at any second. That, plus the creeping boredom that had eclipsed her very soul.

She glanced over her shoulder at her friends and the cluttered pile of top secret paperwork on the desks behind them.

Charlotte let out a huff that sent three pages on the table in front of her flapping into the air. Ray stood on his tiptoes over the copy machine, trying to keep his adorable little alien friend, Meekee, from jumping on the empty ink cartridges.

The filing cabinets were covered in a thick layer of dust. Viv lazily dragged her finger along the top of one, leaving a stark line in its wake. She sighed; the whole room smelled like cobwebs and crushed dreams.

But then again, nothing about this place had really turned out the way Viv had expected. Last week also marked the day her whole life flipped upside down—the day she learned that she wasn't even entirely *human*.

Back when Viv was a baby, her mother had unknowingly mixed alien DNA with Viv's, giving her the powers of the fearsome Roswellian species. Viv hadn't looked in the mirror at all over the last seven days, afraid of what kind of monstrous, green glowing creature might be looking back.

It took everything in her power not to break down and cry in front of her friends every day. But as long as they didn't know the truth about her, she could keep on living life like she used to. All she had to do now was play the role of the obedient intern.

This was supposed to be their summer of fun, but now Viv felt like a freak among her own friends.

All I need to do is stay calm. Avoid anything that could set me off. I need to keep these dumb powers hidden.

"OUCH! Paper cut!" Ray said, gripping his pinky finger like it was about to fall off.

"Meekee!" the pint-size alien peeped. He licked at the back of Ray's hand, trying to help soothe the pain.

"One week ago, you were Mr. Hero. And now look at you," Charlotte said. "I don't know why they don't just let me use the duplicator gauntlets. If I had my clones here with us, we would have been done with this boring paperwork in a day! Geez, some of this stuff is ancient. Look, this folder's from 1996!"

"Ooh, a file from the Archaeology Department. That's a great word. Say it with me, Meekee," Ray instructed. "Ar-kee-aw-la-gee."

Meekee looked up at him with big, determined eyes, wiggling his butt as if he was trying to muster more brainpower.

"Ar . . . Ar-kee . . . Ar-kee . . ." Meekee trailed off.

"You're about to say 'Meekee,' aren't you?"

"Meekee!" the little alien pipped.

"Shouldn't you start him off with something a little easier?" Charlotte said over her shoulder. "Like 'sit'? Or 'stay'? How about 'roll over'?"

"Meekee's not a *puppy*, Charlotte. He's a member of a highly advanced alien species and totally capable of learning a new language. Only a week old, and my boy's already great at one-syllable words. He'll be beating me at Scrabble in no time!"

Charlotte turned her attention to the tiny green blob hopping up and down on the paper tray.

"Meekee, say 'dumb.'"

"Dumb!" the little alien replied.

"Come on!" Ray protested. "Don't teach him that! His English might not be very good now, but just wait until he's fully grown!"

"I've always said the same thing about you, Ray," Charlotte said sweetly as she turned back to her stack.

Viv kept her head down, sorting the papers in front of her in chronological order. As adorable as Meekee's language skills were, they weren't enough to snap her out of this funk. Even working in close quarters with Elijah the whole week hadn't been enough to lift her spirits, partly because he was the one she was most afraid of learning the truth about her. What if he never saw her the same way again? She couldn't risk it.

"Whoa! Guys, look!" Ray said, unclipping an old photograph from the top of a file. "Is this what I think it is?"

He held up the photo beneath the desk lamp as Viv slid over to take a look. There within the Polaroid's white frame was an array of familiar faces.

Charlotte kicked off the wall and rolled her chair over to join them.

"No WAY!" she said. "It's our parents!"

The photo showed Viv's mom, or at least another version of her mom. The streak of gray that normally parted her hair today was instead completely black. She was standing in a row of people leaning against a long table in the employee break room, all holding steamy mugs of tea. Each of the seven smiles in the picture was wide with vibrant laughter. On the back, scribbled in blue ink, was a handwritten description: *Agents Sabrina Holtzmeier, Desmond Frank, Winnie Stenvall, Nicolás Padilla, Ishani Desai, Ernest Becker, and Cassandra Harlow—1999.*

Viv also noticed that Charlotte's parents had their arms draped around each other. And Elijah's dad looked just as handsome as ever. But she didn't recognize anyone else in the photo. Not even the man standing next to her mom, presumably Agent Ernest Becker, who was leaning toward Cassandra with a friendly nudge, both their heads thrown back in laughter.

Agent Becker? Agent Stenvall? Agent Desai? Mom's never mentioned any of these people before. I wonder if they still work here.

"They all look so young!" Charlotte said.

"And so . . ." Viv's voice got caught in her throat.

"Happy?" Ray said.

Viv nodded. He was right. She hadn't seen her mom laugh like that for as long as she could remember. Her head thrown back, without a care in the world. It almost made Viv angry. After everything that had happened last week, Viv needed answers. But she and her mom still hadn't gotten the chance to talk. About anything. Her mom didn't even know about her powers.

Or maybe she *did.*

And if she did know, then why wouldn't she tell me that one day I might wake up with freaky alien abilities? Ugh. Why should I expect anything else? She's always been so secretive.

There was so much Viv didn't know. Starting with the question that had itched at the back of her mind for her entire life.

My dad. Why won't she talk about him? Even Megdar knew more about him than I do!

"Viv?" Ray's voice snapped her out of her trance. "You okay, Viv? You've been pretty quiet."

"Me? I'm totally fine," Viv lied, straightening up in her chair and tossing the picture on the desk. "Just bored of all this paperwork, ya know? This picture might be the most interesting thing I've seen all week."

"You should keep it." Charlotte passed the photo back to Viv.

"What? I can't keep it. This is highly sensitive, classified Area 51 material."

"Looks like a Polaroid to me," Charlotte said.

"No way. I can't take this." Viv rummaged beneath a few piles of manila folders and pulled out a small stapler. With one sharp squeeze of her palm, she attached the photo to the top of the file. "There. Now it won't get lost."

Viv put the paper back into its folder with a sigh and slid the stapler into her pocket, sure she'd need it for a new set of files later. The door slowly creaked open behind her.

"Elijah, where have you been?" Charlotte asked. "We're two filing cabinets away from being done!"

Elijah collapsed into one of the rolling chairs and slid toward his desk.

"Director Harlow had me doing coffee runs again this morning. Agent Snyder? You know, the one who works in the Botany Department? Well, she wanted oat milk in her coffee, so I went to the coffee stand, and they only had soy milk. I got her the coffee with soy milk, but then she tasted it and said it was terrible. So I had to run back to the coffee stand and ask for almond milk. But then she said she was allergic to almonds, so I had to take the VERT Train to the other coffee stand on the north side of the compound and then go all the way back to the Botany Department." Elijah talked until he was out of breath. Charlotte stared at him with wide eyes.

". . . Elijah?" Charlotte said. "Did you drink any of that coffee?"

"Yep! All the coffee that Agent Snyder didn't want. I had to. Otherwise, it would've gone to waste!" Elijah said quickly. "How can you tell?"

"Um, maybe because you're talking like a flying squirrel who just ate a bellyful of jumping beans?"

"Or maybe he's just talking like the world's most reliable intern," Viv said with a smile.

Elijah smiled back and gave her a jittery nod of thanks.

Though the grin he flashed her was warm and sweet, Viv

still wasn't quite sure how to talk with him after the alien attack. She could have sworn they'd shared a moment together on the Roswellians' ship when they thought they'd never see each other again. But she hadn't been able to get him alone for a moment, with all four of them together in the copy room, and he seemed to be pretending it had never happened.

Elijah paced back and forth around the room, energy unabated, before he paused for a moment. He reached over to a small space against the wall.

"Has this been here the whole time?" Elijah said. He banged his hand against another metal cabinet wedged into the corner.

"Aw, man. Seriously? Another one?" Ray said.

Viv watched as Elijah pulled yet another folder out of the new filing cabinet to start digitizing. He reached inside the folder and removed a small, folded-up piece of blue paper.

"What's this?" Elijah asked.

"Probably another Extra-Normal Affairs document. Those are tricky to read," Ray said.

"No, seriously, guys. Look!" Elijah swept his arm across the desk, pushing the other stacks to the side. He unfurled a huge piece of blue paper, so blue that the desk lamp's light reflected like a sparkling sapphire.

"Are you kidding me?" Charlotte said after she leaned over for a peek. "You've been here for ten seconds, and you already found something cool?"

Viv and Ray crowded around. Even Meekee hopped across the stacks of papers to get a better look.

"Whoa."

Viv's eyes scanned the large paper laid out on the desk. She and her friends had gone through thousands of files over the past week. The paper cuts that dotted each of her fingers could attest to that. But there was something missing on this document.

Something not *missing*.

Every single file that they'd encountered was confidential and redacted, crossed through with thick black lines that obscured any interesting or relevant information. But everything on this piece of paper was legible. Clear as day. It only took Viv a second to realize what they were looking at.

"They're blueprints," Viv said. "A map of the compound. The *underground* part."

A map to the deepest, most secretive levels of Area 51. Why isn't this all blacked out?

"Shouldn't this be redacted?" Ray said, echoing Viv's thoughts to a T.

"I guess they forgot?" Elijah said.

"Whoa, look." Charlotte pointed to a small legend in the top right corner. "Is this what I think it is?"

"This has the door codes to every single sector of Area 51 below Level One."

Oh man. This definitely *should have been redacted.*

Something else on the map caught Viv's eye. She traced her finger along the edges until she landed on a circular region of the map ten stories below the desert line.

"What's this here? The *Forbidden Zone*?" Her voice fell to a hush. "I've never heard of that before."

"Probably because it's forbidden," Ray added without a hint of sarcasm.

The four kids stared at it for a long time, the blue light from the document glowing in all of their eyes. They sat for a moment in pure silence.

"I'm gonna file it under 'Miscellaneous,'" Ray said, reaching for the map. Charlotte caught his arm.

"What? No way! We're *definitely* keeping this!"

"Charlotte, no! We can't. This is supposed to be confidential," Viv said. "We shouldn't even be looking at this."

"But it's a map of Area 51? And *we* work here. Shouldn't we know our way around the place?" Charlotte asked, letting the question linger in the air. "What? You think the people who work at Disney World don't know how to get to Space Mountain?"

"I don't think there's a *Forbidden* Zone at Disney World!" Viv replied.

"Actually, you'd be surprised," Ray said. "One time, I wandered into Snow White's dressing room and—"

"We gotta check it out!" Charlotte insisted. "Our parents stuck us in here for the most boring task ever. Obviously, they don't care what we do as long as we're out of the way. Nobody needs to know. We can run down there, see what's up, and then run back before anyone notices."

Ray cautiously picked up the map as if the paper itself was radioactive.

"If we get caught with this, we could get in serious trouble."

KNOCK! KNOCK!

A knuckle tapped at the door in two sharp beats.

"AH!" Ray yelped. The map flew out of his hands.

"AH!" Meekee repeated cheerfully.

"Hide it!" Viv whispered as Charlotte ferociously folded it back up.

"I'm trying!" In one quick swoop, Charlotte picked Meekee up off the table and plopped him down on top of the folded-up square of blue paper.

"Meekee?"

"Stay right there, Meekee! Don't move!" Viv commanded. "Stay!"

"Stay!" Meekee parroted back.

"Good boy, Meekee!"

"Guys," Ray exclaimed. "He's not a puppy!"

The door scraped open and a looming figure filled the doorframe. Viv's fear was instantly replaced with a new feeling . . .

Dread.

CHAPTER TWO

"Director Harlow!" Elijah smiled wide. "Good afternoon!"

Viv's mom, tall and proud, stepped into the room, her heels clacking on the cold concrete floor.

"Good afternoon, Elijah. Thanks again for handling the coffee this morning. I heard Agent Snyder gave you quite the runaround."

"Oh, not a problem! Happy to help in any way I can." Elijah chuckled nervously, his hands still fidgeting in his lap. "What, um, what can we do you for?"

"I want you all to meet someone!"

Director Harlow stepped to her left and pushed the door wide open. Behind the frame stood a new figure—a sight Viv was certainly not expecting to see.

It was a girl. Not a woman but a girl. She was tall and thin, wearing a tidy green dress with a bow around the collar. A stream of pin-straight auburn hair fell to her waist.

"Kids, this is Joanna Kim. Joanna, these are the new

interns—my daughter, Vivian, and her very capable friends Charlotte, Elijah, and Ray."

Viv was shocked. For the past week, her entire world had been full of adults. Seeing anybody under five and a half feet tall at the base was unusual unless you found yourself in the copy room where she and her friends had been relegated.

"Um, Director Harlow? I thought Area 51 was done with Take Your Kids to Work Day?" Charlotte said.

"Oh no, no." Their boss laughed. "Joanna here is Area 51's newest Einstein Fellow."

"Einstein Fellow?" Ray's ears perked up at his favorite physicist's name.

"Yes, it's an outreach program we've been sponsoring for decades. Each year, the award goes to an eligible scientist who's demonstrated excellence in their field. We choose from thousands of brilliant minds, but this year, our winner happened to be, well . . . a bit younger than we expected." She smiled down at Joanna, who smiled right back.

"Joanna here is a prodigy in all things biology and organic robotics. She's been upstairs working with me in the main hall this morning. Even though she's only been here for a few hours, she's already helped Lieutenant Padilla and I solve a pesky engineering problem with the new Draco-Drone."

Viv's eyes narrowed, and she felt her hands clench into fists by her side.

A new kid genius? Working with Mom while we're stuck

down here? You've got to be kidding me.

"How old are you?" Ray asked.

"Fourteen." Joanna smiled, her perfectly straight teeth gleaming white.

"I'll get out of your hair and let you all get acquainted. Don't want to bring down the vibe!" Director Harlow added with a chuckle. "And I know you interns are almost finished, but don't work through lunch. Today, we have an extra-special buffet that you don't want to miss!"

The director turned toward the door and twisted the knob—

"Stay!" Meekee chirped again.

Director Harlow spun around toward the sound, and Viv's eyes darted to the folded piece of paper beneath Meekee's butt.

"Oh, Meekee!" She laughed. "Ray, you must be doing a great job teaching him to speak. He's learning so fast!"

"Stay! Stay!" Meekee echoed.

"That's so sweet. I'm afraid I must get going, little guy."

"Dumb!" Meekee replied.

Director Harlow laughed once more and continued walking. "I expect you four to give Joanna a warm welcome!"

Director Harlow turned on her heels and shut the door behind her. Joanna stepped into her place. Charlotte, Elijah, and Ray shared a collective sigh of relief, but Viv's eyes were fixed on the mysterious new girl, standing in front of them.

"Hi, there! You must be Viv. Nice to meet you." Joanna extended her hand warmly.

"Einstein Fellow, huh? How'd you win that?" Viv asked, turning back toward the desk and trying to suppress the edge in her voice.

"I'll show you!" Joanna said, gently patting the pocket of her crisp dress.

From the velvety fabric, a bright white metal head popped out. It was a small head, no bigger than a plum, topped with two beady eyes and long, wiry whiskers. Connected to that head was a skinny body made of smooth, white steel plates. If Viv didn't know any better, she'd say it was a weasel. A mechanical weasel.

The little metal creature slithered up Joanna's arm and perched itself on top of her shoulder.

"This is FuRo." Joanna patted the miniature droid on the head as it nuzzled against her chin. "She's the reason I'm here."

"Whoa!" Ray's eyes lit up at the technical masterpiece in front of him. He always appreciated a good invention.

"Wow. You made that?" Elijah asked.

"Yep! Built her in the lab this spring. She's a fully automated robotic ferret with integrated artificial intelligence and all sorts of extra features."

A ferret? She made a robot ferret? Big whoop. I battled a dinosaur.

A low growl emerged from Ray's desk. It was Meekee, flattening himself like a hissing kitten. Something about this robotic ferret clearly ruffled him.

"Dumb!" the tiny alien peeped.

"Meekee!" Ray scolded. "Where are your manners, young man?"

Within an instant of noticing him, FuRo leapt off Joanna's shoulders and soared through the air, landing perfectly on the desk, inches from Meekee's face. They sniffed each other for a moment before breaking into an all-out wrestling match.

"Meekee! Stop that right now!" Ray howled.

Joanna laughed. "Oh, they'll be okay! FuRo's harmless. Just having some fun."

While Viv watched the two pocket-size creatures brawl, her ears homed in on the conversation happening behind her.

"And you must be Elijah, right?" Joanna said. "I think you ran by me this morning on your way to the Botany Department."

"Oh yeah." Elijah ruffled the hair behind his head. "Sorry about that. I should've introduced myself."

"Don't worry. You looked busy. I remember thinking, 'Wow! Whoever he is, that guy's fast!'"

Joanna curled her lips into a smile, and her giggle rang out like a sparrow's call. Viv's heart tensed up at the sound.

She's flirting *with him. Already?*

And that was when she felt it: the burning heat boiling behind her eyes. It was the same sensation she had felt last week when her powers exploded out of her . . . when she accidentally hurt Elijah. Viv shut her eyes tight, trying to fight off the pull of her unwanted abilities.

CLANG!

The sound startled Viv and nearly everyone else in the room. It was Charlotte. She flipped the deadbolt on the door and whirled around to face them.

"Enough chitchat. What are we gonna do with this map?"

"Charlotte!" Ray cried, nervously glancing over at Joanna.

"What?" Charlotte defended. "Joanna, you're a genius, right? Why don't we let her decide?"

"You found a map?" Joanna said.

Viv's skin tingled. Something about this felt wrong. They'd just met her. Could she be trusted?

I'm sure Little Miss Perfect will turn us in the second she gets back upstairs.

"Let me take a look," Joanna said, extending her hand.

Viv noticed her fingers, covered in shiny silver rings that perfectly matched her freshly painted manicure. Joanna spread the map out onto the desk and glanced over it with lightning speed.

"Ooh, the *Forbidden Zone*?" Joanna smiled. "That sounds cool."

"That's exactly what I said!" Charlotte folded her arms across her chest.

"But it's supposed to be confidential!" Ray said, trying to pry Meekee away from the headlock FuRo had him in.

"What do you think we should do, Joanna?" Elijah asked.

She flashed him a quick grin before looking back at the big blue document.

"I think . . ." She twirled a lock of smooth hair around her fingers. "Why work at Area 51 if you're not up for a little adventure?"

"Yeah! Now that's what I'm talking about!" Charlotte shot her hands up in victory.

Elijah nodded in agreement. Viv felt like she was going to throw up. She wrapped her hand around the stapler in her pocket and squeezed hard, wishing it was the trigger on her combat suit.

Stay calm . . . Stay calm . . .

Trilling chimes echoed through the intercom speaker.

"That's the lunch bell! Guys, please!" Ray said, out of breath, finally breaking Meekee free from the scuffle and tucking him into his shirt pocket. "Let's just file it away for now and get some food!"

"It'll only take a second, Ray," Charlotte said, already half-way out the door. "No one's gonna notice if we're a few files behind schedule. They're all busy doing actually cool stuff."

"But Director Harlow said there's a special buffet today!" Ray whined.

"Come on, Ray. I promise we won't run into Snow White."

CHAPTER
THREE

Itchy edges of white lab coats brushed against Viv as dozens of Area 51 employees made their way to the dining hall. She and her friends clung to the wall, squeezing by each pair of chatting adults headed in the opposite direction.

The group kept their heads down until, finally, they made it to an empty stretch of the compound free of any other employees: Internal Staircase Zeta.

They tiptoed down the seemingly endless concrete stairwell, swinging past landing after landing as they spiraled into the depths of Area 51. With Joanna and Charlotte leading the way, their noses buried in the big blue map, they kept the group at a brisk pace. Viv could already feel a blister forming.

"We should've taken the VERT Train," Elijah said with a huff.

"You've got legs, don't you?" Charlotte called over her shoulder.

A deep voice echoed through the stairwell from above.

"What are you kids doing down here?" it called out.

Oh no. We've been caught.

Viv twisted her head up to see Agent Vega, one of the US military liaisons at the base, leaning over the railing. A thick black mustache crept across his upper lip like a fuzzy caterpillar. He had somewhat of a reputation at the compound for being strict and never smiling. Just in the last week alone, Viv had seen Agent Vega yell at one of the nuclear engineers for improperly recycling a cardboard box.

Joanna took a spry step forward.

"Agent Vega, hello!" She smiled. FuRo wrapped herself around Joanna's neck like a mechanical scarf.

"Oh, Joanna! Good to see you again." Agent Vega relaxed his posture at the sight of her. "Shouldn't you all be at lunch?"

They know each other? But she's only been here for a day!

"Yes, we're headed there shortly," Joanna assured. "Director Harlow asked me to take the interns down to the cyanobacterium lab to retrieve a few samples of *Synechococcus* PCC 7942 to mix with the cellulose synthase genes from *Gluconacetobacter xylinus* to produce extracellular noncrystalline cellulose for an electrode we're designing."

Agent Vega nodded, the woolly insect below his nose bouncing with every tilt. But Viv could tell. Whatever Joanna said went right over his head. And as much as Viv didn't want to admit, it went over her head, too.

"Working during your lunch break? Now that's the kind of discipline I like to see!"

Agent Vega leaned farther over the railing, examining Joanna and FuRo with curiosity. He lowered his already baritone voice an octave lower.

"You know, if you ever get tired of all this science nonsense, there's a wonderful apprenticeship program at the Department of Defense for bright young minds like yours. We'd love to have you. You'd even have your own office at the Pentagon."

"That's very kind, Agent Vega." Joanna smiled. "But I actually love the work we're doing here. And it's nice having the interns with me, too."

Viv narrowed her eyes.

Geez. The way she said "interns" makes it sound like we work for her.

"I understand." Agent Vega clasped his hands together with a dry thwack. "Well, something to think about, Joanna. Carry on!"

Agent Vega clacked the metal tips of his dress shoes on the floor and continued up the stairs. Once he rounded the next flight, stepped onto the landing, and closed the door behind him, the four interns looked to Joanna with wide eyes.

"What?" Joanna shrugged. "Let's get moving! We're almost there!"

Each step farther into the underground corridors sent a rush of adrenaline through Viv. As much as she was morally against this unauthorized excursion, she had to admit . . .

Even I want to know what's down here.

After a few more minutes of stairs, the five kids rounded

one more landing and were practically blinded by the cherry-red door that marked the lowest point of the stairwell.

Painted across the titanium, dark crimson lettering announced exactly what they were looking for:

"THE FORBIDDEN ZONE"

A smaller line of text just below:

"Clearance Level Ten Required"

Viv glanced down at the intern badge clipped to her lanyard. It read a much lower number.

Clearance level one . . . We're definitely *not supposed to be here.*

"Guys." Ray gulped. "There's still time to make it to lunch if we hurry back now."

Joanna turned to face the four of them, the badge on her hip swaying in the red glowing light from the door. Viv quickly homed in on the distinctly different clearance level.

"You're level *nine*?" Viv asked.

"Yep." Joanna smiled. "I guess being an Einstein Fellow has its perks."

"Your level nine plus our level one equals level ten. That's good enough for me!" Charlotte unfurled the blue map.

Before Viv could say anything, Charlotte had already cracked her knuckles and placed her fingers on the security panel by the doorknob.

"Okay! Here goes nothing."

The security code was a rambling, motley assortment of letters, numbers, and shapes. Charlotte typed a dozen keys.

Then another dozen. And then another.

"Seriously, how long is this security code?" Ray fidgeted, hopping from one foot to the other.

"Turns out, it's the same number of times you've picked your nose, Ray." Charlotte smiled.

"Ha ha. Very funny," Ray said.

In unison, Elijah and Joanna cocked their heads back and laughed. Viv felt her jaw tighten. Seeing them in sync made her want to puke.

I can be funny, too.

Viv leaned over Charlotte's shoulder, pretending to read the security code on the map.

"You missed a two," Viv said.

"Aw shoot, really?" Charlotte's eyes got wide.

"Ha, made you look!" Viv smirked.

Charlotte just stared at her best friend. Nobody was laughing.

"That's not funny, Viv. I almost started over."

Viv chuckled nervously and stepped back again. She tucked her hair behind her ears, trying to keep from blushing.

"What do you think is back there?" Ray squeaked.

"My guess?" Elijah whispered. "Elvis. Or Tupac."

Charlotte dialed in one last symbol, and the security panel trilled five short beeps. The door unlatched with a thud.

Holy crud. It worked.

Ever so slowly, Charlotte twisted the knob on the door.

And as it opened, Viv couldn't believe her eyes . . .

CHAPTER
FOUR

"More stairs?" Elijah asked.

Behind the big red door was yet another staircase, descending into complete, menacing darkness. Viv stared at the stairs and the stairs stared back at her with a stare that made her not want to go down the stairs.

"More freaking stairs? Maybe that's why it's forbidden," Charlotte added. "Because you'll burn too many calories trying to get back up."

The five kids stood frozen for a moment until Joanna lifted her foot and hovered it over the first step.

"Wait!" Ray stuck out his arm. "What if this leads into, like, a fiery dungeon?"

"A fiery dungeon? You think it'd be pitch-black if it was a fiery dungeon?" Joanna said.

"Ray's right. We don't know what's down there," Viv said. "Who even knows if the stairs are safe to walk down? Why would they keep them locked up behind a big, bolted forbidden door? What if it's a radioactive staircase?"

"It's not," Joanna said. "FuRo has a built-in Geiger counter. We'd know if it was dangerous."

And down the stairs they went. Footstep after footstep, until eventually they saw the faintest hints of red-and-white light.

Joanna was the first to hit the bottom landing, a concrete floor painted the same striking crimson as the front door. Then Charlotte. Then Elijah. Then Viv, dragging Ray along.

"It's a . . . ?" Ray's voice trailed off at the spectacle laid out before them.

Viv felt a familiar sense of excitement bloom inside her.

A zoo?

Stretched out in a semicircle in front of them, dozens of strange creatures all on display behind large plates of glass walls—glass so clear, it looked like nothing separated them from the animals but pure oxygen.

Viv took a cautious step forward toward a marshy, wet enclosure. A few feet beyond where she stood, swimming between the cypress and tupelo roots that dipped into the swamp water, was a type of animal she'd never seen before.

It was a group of dark green, enormous salamander-like reptiles. They glided through the mud, each about two feet long. Spiny scales spilled down their backs into long tails like an alligator's. A set of vibrating gills surrounded their faces. They reminded Viv of those swimming iguanas she'd seen in documentaries on the Galápagos Islands.

And they weren't the only odd creatures. In the enclosure to their right, perched atop a sturdy Joshua tree, was the most magnificent bird Viv had ever seen. Wings stretched out in its personal patch of sunlight, the beast looked like a gigantic brown eagle. Bolts of blue electricity, almost akin to lightning, extended from the tips of its tail feathers, crackling and popping in the arid air.

The bird peered at the curious kids, focusing its sapphire-blue eyes down the barrel of its sharp beak directly at Viv.

"Whoa." Elijah's voice nearly cracked. "What . . . what are these things?"

"They're cryptids." Joanna's eyes shimmered. A smile crept up at the corners of her mouth.

"Cryptids?" Charlotte parroted back. "You're telling me all these animals own Bitcoin?"

"They're creatures believed to have existed for centuries but haven't been proven by science yet." Joanna took a step forward, toward the king-size eagle. "I can't believe they're all real."

A small touch screen embedded beside the glass barrier blinked to life as her motion was detected.

In red letters, the screen lit up with the bird's information:
CRYPTOZOOLOGICAL SUBJECT NO. 11238
ARAPAHO THUNDERBIRD
CLASSIFICATION: ANCIENT ACCIPITRIFORMES
STATUS: FORBIDDEN IN NORTH AMERICA

"Forbidden in North America?" Joanna's jaw tightened.

"What does that mean? Is that why they're locked away down here?"

"Look! There are a bunch more!" Charlotte said. FuRo hopped off Joanna's shoulder and bounded down the circular hall. Elijah followed suit.

"Ray, come on!" he said, tugging at their reluctant friend's sleeve.

Viv looked back up at the long stairwell they'd descended from. Faintly, the light from the open door at the top of the stairs cut through the darkness. She was glad they'd left the heavy door open. Getting locked down here with all these potentially dangerous animals wasn't her idea of fun.

The kids crowded around another smooth glass panel. Inside, tall pine trees extended beyond their view up through the ceiling. Patches of half-melted snow gathered around fallen piles of needles. Elijah approached with caution.

"Does this say what I think it says?" Elijah asked.

The touch screen on the wall beside the glass flashed:

CRYPTOZOOLOGICAL SUBJECT NO. 49722

AMERICAN WEREWOLVES

CLASSIFICATION: LYCANTHROPES

STATUS: FORBIDDEN IN NORTH AMERICA AND LONDON

Viv folded her arms across her chest, feeling goose bumps rise on her skin, suddenly colder than before. Behind her, Ray and Meekee sunk closer into the wall.

"Yep. That says 'werewolves,'" Charlotte said.

Elijah tried to peek around the trees for a better look.

"But I don't see anything?"

"Look, what's that?" Charlotte said, pointing toward the roof of the enclosure.

Nestled between the climbing pine trunks in the ceiling, an iron porthole was slid open.

"Maybe they climbed up through there," Charlotte offered.

"Yeah, but *where* is 'up there'?" Viv said.

Charlotte reviewed the map in her hands.

"From the looks of this, I'd say we're directly below the terrarium. Maybe half a mile or so underground."

The puzzle pieces suddenly fell into place inside Viv's mind.

"Remember the dinosaurs in the terrarium? I bet those little openings in the ceiling are each connected to a different sector of the terrarium, a habitat that's perfectly suited to each creature. This must be where the scientists keep them for observation."

"Then why call this place the Forbidden Zone?"

"These animals . . . ," Viv said. "I think they're all forbidden *outside* of Area 51. And that's why they're keeping them here, away from the world."

"I don't understand why any creature should be forbidden," Joanna said. "If they're meant to be in the natural world, why would anybody need to lock them up?"

Ray's voice echoed in from farther around the circle.

"*Chupacabra*? What's that?"

It was rare for Ray to find a word he didn't know. He and Meekee knelt down by the glass enclosure. The tiny green fuzz on Meekee's head stood up straight, making his petite frame look a few millimeters bigger.

A high-pitched warning growl rumbled from the little alien.

"Meekee? What's wrong, buddy? You see something?" Ray asked, gently patting his small companion on the head. Meekee's gaze never shifted. Something in there had caught his attention.

And whatever it is, Meekee doesn't like it.

Viv inspected the habitat. Dry, sandy soil stretched beneath rows of sunbaked crops, not unlike the miles of dead farmland that spread throughout Nevada during bad droughts.

I don't see it—

Two massive red eyes blinked open from between parched stalks of corn. A sharp inhale cut though Viv's nostrils. She squinted into the shadows. Suddenly, terrifying details of the creature's silhouette began to untangle. A long, lashing tongue flicked back and forth across snarling teeth. Saliva sprayed with every whip. The droplets fell to the ground with a hiss, sending steam rising from the afflicted spots of sand.

"Let's uh . . . keep going," Viv said.

The group of kids trailed farther around the circular zoo, oohing and ahhing, until Joanna stopped in her tracks. She leaned down in front of an enclosure.

"Wow," Joanna said, pressing her hands up to the glass.

Inside, a group of wide-eyed rabbits shivered beneath the wildflowers of prairie grass. They were adorable. If it weren't for the huge, buck-style antlers sprouting from the top of their heads, Viv would want one as a pet.

"These are jackalopes . . . I can't believe they actually exist!"

Viv scoffed under her breath. "Looks like someone glued antlers on rabbits to me."

"Exactly! *Lepus timidus* mixed with ungulate *Cervidae* DNA. Do you know what kind of impact this could have on the world of biological genetics?"

Viv and Charlotte exchanged a look.

More Joanna genius-speak.

"I'm gonna go in there," Joanna said, stepping up to the glass. "Get a better look at the little guys."

"What?" Viv said. "No way. None of us should go in there."

"Why not?" Joanna asked.

"We don't know what those things could do! What if you get hurt?"

"Oh, they're harmless." Joanna smiled. "Like you said, just some rabbits with antlers."

"Hah! You did say that, Viv," Charlotte said with a shrug.

"I know what I said!" Viv snapped back.

"Can't this wait until after lunch?" Ray asked. "Come on, guys. We wanted to find out what was down here, and we did that. Let's head back before we get in trouble. Plus, need I remind you? Buffet!"

"You really want to climb down all those stairs back here again?" Joanna asked. "Charlotte, hand me the map."

Charlotte gazed down at the secret document in her hand, then back up between Viv and Joanna.

Don't do it, Char.

"Charlotte, come on," Joanna urged, sticking out her hand. "We came all this way, didn't we? Those poor jackalopes are stuck in there all day. I'm sure a little stimulation couldn't hurt."

Charlotte passed her the map. Viv's heart sank in her chest.

Joanna punched the twenty digits into the touch screen with lightning speed. The glass that had been separating them slid up in one smooth glide as Joanna passed the map back to Charlotte. Ray gasped. Viv's disappointment transformed into fear.

It's that easy to get in there? That's what's separating us from werewolves? From that Chupacabra?

The whole place suddenly felt way more dangerous now.

The air inside the jackalopes' enclosure was torrid and sandy. Each of the rabbits sat up on their hind legs, noses twitching in the breeze of their little open chunk of prairie.

Joanna took a tiny step into the enclosure. Then another. And then a twig snapped beneath her shoe.

The herd exploded out of the enclosure. Each rabbit sprinted between the legs of the dumbfounded kids who had accidentally released them.

"Stay!" Meekee howled.

A millisecond of panic paralyzed everyone as nine of the

ten jackalopes took off at breakneck speed around the yet unexplored curve of the circular zoo.

"See?!" Viv shouted. "I told you not to go in there!"

"This is it! We're gonna get fired from our unpaid internship!" Ray looked like he was going to faint. Meekee tried to fan Ray's face with his nubby little alien legs, without success.

"What do we do? What do we do?!" Elijah said.

"Everybody calm down," Joanna insisted. "FuRo is programmed with a foolproof rabbit call. We'll lure them back into their little section and close the glass again."

"You think FuRo's rabbit call will work on mythological creatures?"

"I don't see why not!" Joanna said. And with that, she and FuRo took off after the herd, a strange, high-pitched squealing sound emitting from the robotic ferret.

Viv watched as the lone jackalope, the one who'd sprinted out to the left instead of to the right, scurried out of sight.

"Wait! What about that one?" Viv called out.

But she was too late. With Joanna leading the way, her friends had taken off around the opposite curve of the circle, chasing after the bulk of the sprinting jackalopes.

Great! Guess I'll go alone.

Viv's feet carried her as fast as they could. She picked up speed past the Chupacabra and darted beyond the werewolves until the giant thunderbird was back in sight. Finally, she caught up to the lone hare, running back toward the entrance . . .

toward the staircase where they had come in . . .

Toward the open *door!*

"Shoot!" Viv shouted.

The jackalope heard her outburst and looked for an escape. It leapt up the first stair. Then the second. And the third.

Viv had to act fast.

Joanna did this. She's gonna get us in so much trouble. The second that rabbit's loose in the compound, we're all gonna get fired.

Suddenly, Viv felt the tingling start in her fingertips, the burning that she'd tried to suppress all week. The anger boiled behind her eyes, her frustration breaking down the emotional walls she'd built up. It rattled through her arms and coated her skin with a glistening green blaze.

Before she knew it, the jackalope on the steps was suspended in midair, a glowing field of green light shrouding the quivering hare as it yelped.

". . . Viv?"

A hesitant voice came from behind her. Viv's eyes slammed shut. The jackalope hit the floor and skittered down the stairs, running through Viv's legs and back toward its enclosure.

Charlotte's jaw fell open.

Oh no. She saw me. She saw my powers!

Viv's brain felt like it was in overdrive. She wasn't ready to reveal her secret yet, even to her best friend. But what could she do? Her hands shook, and as they did, she felt the outline of the stapler in in her pocket from where she'd stashed it earlier.

There's no way this could work . . . could it?

Quickly, Viv pulled out the stapler and turned to show it to her incredulous friend.

"You're not gonna believe this, Charlotte, but this stapler?" Viv choked out. "Turns out, it's actually a high-tech levitation device. The designers must've disguised it as a stapler so it wouldn't fall into the wrong hands."

Charlotte's shoulders were practically glued to her ears, her eyebrows pulled up in a confused arch.

"The . . . the *stapler* did that? The stapler lifted that rabbit into the air?" she asked. "And made your eyes glow green?"

Viv bit down hard on her tongue and managed a nod. Instead of her despised alien abilities, she felt tears welling up behind her eyes.

Please, Charlotte. Please believe me.

Charlotte looked down at the stapler in Viv's hand and then back up.

Finally, after what felt like an eternity, Charlotte let out a sigh. "Well . . . I guess I've seen crazier stuff here than a levitational stapler."

"Viv! Charlotte!" It was Elijah, his distant voice coming from around the bend of the hallway. "We got 'em all!"

Without another word, Charlotte turned away from Viv, dutifully jogging back toward the jackalope enclosure.

Whew!

CHAPTER FIVE

The dining hall at Area 51 zipped with activity. The room itself was already impressively large in its own right, located just south of the main hall. Long tables saddled with equally long benches created a perfect place for the nation's foremost scientific minds to gather, eat, and share their enthusiasm over a first-class meal.

Viv and her friends had been eating lunch there every day for the past week, taking up one of the smaller tables near the back of the room, staying out of the way of the higher levels and their confidential conversations.

But today, instead of new experiments and top secret whispering, the focus seemed to be on the food.

In place of the usual salad bar and quinoa bowls, the cafeteria was filled with extraterrestrial fruits and alien vegetables. Placards labeled the array of colorful shapes and foods Viv had never seen before. She and her friends picked up a plate and filed in at the back of the bustling line.

Viv's muscles ached from the hundreds of stairs they had

climbed back up from the Forbidden Zone. But the pain in her legs couldn't compare to the pounding in her head. After Joanna and FuRo rounded up all the jackalopes and got them into their enclosure again, the kids hustled back to the cafeteria in near silence. Charlotte would barely make eye contact with her. As much as she'd hoped the stapler defense worked, Viv couldn't help but feel like her best friend suddenly knew her deepest, darkest secret.

Viv stared as she passed by a vat full of bubbling gray sludge. It was possibly one of the most disgusting things she'd ever seen, and she'd seen Charlotte try to floss her teeth with her toes. But then, coming from the same tray as the muck, an unexpected aroma tickled Viv's nose. Almost like warm apples and cinnamon.

"Pretty cool, huh?" Agent Snyder, the botanist, stood over the table, sliding a huge tray marked "K2-18b Broccoli" into the row of strange foods. "That's a new blend of atmospheric water from Dimidium mixed with dust we found on the Swift-Tuttle Comet. It's delicious."

She scooped a spoonful of the muck onto Viv's plate with a stomach-churning splatter.

"I promise you're gonna love it. Oh, and you must try the Martian sweet potatoes. Only the best for our little heroes!"

Before Viv could protest, two oblong, neon orange lumps ended up beside the goop already threatening to spill over the edge of her plate.

"Here! Some for you, too, Elijah." Agent Snyder zeroed in on the next victim in line.

Elijah's eyes twitched as he passed her, clearly still traumatized from her particularly tricky coffee order this morning.

Once their dishes were full of interstellar delicacies, Viv and her friends slid into their usual table, trying their best to blend in as employees who perfectly follow all the rules.

"Guys, check this out," Ray said, pointing to what appeared to be a pile of nose-shaped dumplings, complete with nostrils. He split one open with his fork. Green slime oozed out.

"Ew! What the heck is that?" Elijah asked.

"They're fluberries from planet Gliese 667 Cc," Ray said, popping one into his mouth with a gloopy munch. "They're so good!"

Elijah held back a gag while Charlotte took a wary bite of the gray sludge.

"For somebody who seems afraid of pretty much everything, I can't believe you're out here eating noses," Joanna added.

"Guess you could say I'm a picky eater," Ray said, squishing another gooey nose berry against the roof of his mouth.

"Just wait until those dumb space coconuts are ready," Viv said, trying to coax a smile out of Charlotte. Nothing. "Remember? From last week?"

"Oh no," Charlotte said, disregarding Viv entirely. Her voice dropped down to a whisper. She frantically patted at the pockets on her skirt.

"What's wrong?" Elijah said.

"Guys." Her face started to lose its color. "I can't find the map."

You've gotta be kidding.

Viv shot her eyes over the table at Ray and Elijah. Ray's eyes looked like the size of Frisbees behind his glasses.

"We just had it!" Elijah said. "How'd you lose it?"

"I don't know, but it's not here!" Charlotte said. Meekee, who had dived into Charlotte's side pocket to aid in the search, popped his head out and gave a shrug.

"Well, that's just great, Charlotte!" Ray said. "You're gonna get us all fired. Aw, geez. I told you it was a bad idea!"

"Calm down, Ray," Charlotte said. "We'll just go and pick it up."

"You must've dropped it while we were chasing the jacka-lopes," Joanna offered.

"Or maybe it's somewhere on the stairs?" Elijah suggested.

"What do we do?" Ray said. "What do we do?!"

"I guess we'll have to go back before we leave tonight," Joanna said. "Pick it up before anyone notices it."

"Isn't the spread today great?" Director Harlow slid onto the bench right next to Joanna.

Everybody at the table tensed up the second their boss appeared. "There's a whole universe of delicious cuisine out there," she continued, oblivious to their stress. "Makes you real-ize just how limited we are with the food on our home planet."

Viv wanted to curl up in a Meekee-size ball and roll home. Everything felt like it was spiraling out of control, and the last thing she wanted to do was face her mother. But considering that there was a chance Charlotte knew the truth about her secret powers, it was now or never. She had to confront her mom once and for all and get the answers she so desperately needed.

What really happened? And why didn't you ever tell me?

Viv was about to tug on her shirtsleeve and ask for a private word when—

"I can't thank you all enough for the hard work this past week." Director Harlow's voice turned sincere. "I know filing, copying, and shredding documents isn't the most glamorous work, but the way you four have stayed focused has been a true testament to your discipline."

The interns exchanged a long, uncomfortable glance. Viv swallowed down a bite of Martian sweet potato alongside her guilt.

We stole a map, sneaked into the Forbidden Zone, accidentally released ten mythological creatures into the compound, and then lost the map. How's that for discipline?

"Tell you what." Director Harlow smiled. "As a special treat for finishing all that work in record time, I'd like to invite you guys to our Game Night tonight."

"Game Night?" Charlotte asked, licking her plate clean of the sweet-smelling gray muck. "You're telling me all of these agents and scientists get together to play Monopoly every month?"

Director Harlow laughed. "Something like that. It's a monthly celebration and somewhat of a tradition here."

"Can I come, too?" Joanna asked.

"Are you kidding? Of course!" Director Harlow gave her newest protégé a smile. "In fact, Joanna, if you're done eating, I'd love your help on a new project we've been contracted for by the National Park Service."

"I'd be happy to help," Joanna said, throwing her napkin onto the table and standing up in one swift motion.

"Wonderful," Director Harlow said, matching Joanna's upright stance. She turned to the interns. "Once you've finished up with the last of the filing, come find us in the main hall, and I'll escort you to Game Night. See you soon!"

Viv watched the back of her mom's hair sway with each step as she walked away with the girl wonder. All Viv could do was swirl her spoon around in the gloopy, gray mush.

CHAPTER SIX

Game Night at Area 51 was nothing like Viv had expected. After they finished up the last of their paperwork for the day, the interns followed Director Harlow and Joanna into a frenzied arena, another gigantic space Viv had yet to discover at the base. Every day, the compound proved to be bigger than she could've ever imagined.

"Quick, come in, come in. I told them to start without us," Director Harlow whispered.

"What is this place?" Viv asked aloud.

"It's our weapons-testing facility. But on the last Friday of each month, it doubles as a sort of . . . coliseum, I suppose you could call it."

Rows of auditorium-style seats flanked either side of a massive pool of water—the kind of thing you'd see killer whales swimming in at SeaWorld. The rest of Area 51's staff was already there, filling the seats like fans at a major sporting event. Years ago, when she was much younger, Viv's mom had taken her to a minor league hockey game. Viv complained that the ice rink was too cold and too loud, and they never went again.

But now, under the lights of this stadium, she felt exhilarated.

Rising out of the water like ancient Grecian columns, two narrow platforms towered above the waves, each with a single person standing on top.

She recognized one immediately. It was Agent Beth Broderick, a computer specialist in the Department of Vehicle Technology. On Viv's third day, she learned that Broderick was somewhat of a celebrity at the base for singlehandedly designing the AVA system that operated all of Area 51's self-driving trucks. She was one of the older employees at the compound, having worked here since long before Viv's mom.

Viv squinted across the open space at the other pedestal. The opposing player was Agent Gabriel O'Malley, a large, lumbering member of the Linguistics Unit who studied intergalactic languages. She'd met him in passing once on her way to the bathroom. A nice guy, normally, but tonight, he brandished a luminescent whip made out of swelling bands of red light.

The two were engaged in a spectacular battle, a display Viv had never seen before. Other employees and agents hollered and clapped with every move.

A loud, booming voice vibrated over the arena's PA system, nearly rattling the seats as Viv and her friends plopped down.

"O'Malley's infinity whip was inches from Broderick, but she held steady! Oh! And Broderick fires back! A spot-on throw!"

"That voice . . . It's so familiar," Ray said.

"It's your dad, genius!" Charlotte shouted, her Australian accent coming out in full force. She pointed up toward a small observation room suspended above the top row of the auditorium, where Mr. Al Mond sat behind a microphone, a smile spread wide enough across his face for Viv to see even at this distance.

"Oh yeah! I KNEW I recognized that voice from somewhere."

"Normally, Mr. Yates would serve as our announcer for the games, but . . ." Director Harlow cleared her throat. "Now that he's locked up after what he did last week, well, we've had to improvise a bit. Your dad offered to fill in for now, Ray."

The whip wrapped around Agent Broderick's ankle. With one hefty yank, Agent O'Malley pulled Agent Broderick to her backside, impacting the platform with a loud clang.

"My goodness! I've never seen such a thing!" Mr. Mond's voice boomed through the arena. "And O'Malley with a devastating move on Broderick! Can he pull it off?"

"What are they doing? Trying to kill each other?" Joanna asked.

"The rules are actually quite simple," Director Harlow said. "Each participant gets to choose one item to take up onto that platform with them. Could be a weapon, could be an experiment they're working on, I've seen all sorts of things in this arena. Using only that one item, they must knock their opponent off into the water."

"And whoever's left standing wins?" Joanna said.

"Exactly."

Viv pursed her lips into a thin line.

She should be telling this to me. *Not Joanna.*

Viv tried to steel her envy and focused her eyes again on the platforms. Perhaps it was just a trick of the light, but Viv could swear . . .

"Are the platforms getting *smaller*?"

"Ah, yes. I forgot to mention—the platforms get smaller," Director Harlow said with a devious smile. "They shrink an inch every ten seconds. You know, for the sake of time. We don't have all day."

A rush of nerves shot through Viv's spine. Even though she wasn't the one up there, the idea of facing an onslaught by a high-powered, futuristic weapon while standing thirty feet in the air was enough to make her shudder.

"Is it safe?" Viv asked in response, without considering the implication.

Director Harlow's head snapped toward her daughter.

"Of course it's safe," her mother responded, somewhat offended. "This arena has a remote network that switches every piece of technology into safety protocol mode. It's one of the reasons we test weapons in here. You think I'd ever endanger my employees? What kind of director would I be?"

Right. Maybe the same kind of director who would lie to a powerful alien, keep him and his species locked up for years, and inject yourself with his stolen DNA?

But Viv held her tongue.

Mr. Mond's voice reverberated through the arena as Agent Broderick sent an L-shaped object cutting through the air.

"And Agent O'Malley is slammed once again by the hyper boomerang!"

Looking a bit more desperate, Agent O'Malley lashed out his wrist again, sending his whip slicing through the air.

With lightning speed, the hyper boomerang impacted the whip, causing the glowing red light to wrap around the boomerang's elbow as it continued on its path. The force began dragging O'Malley, who refused to let go of his whip and his chances to win. He dug in his heels and slid for a few feet before finally tumbling off the platform in a mass of flailing limbs. O'Malley's body slapped into the water hard enough that Viv felt the stinging on her own stomach.

"And that's that," Director Harlow said.

She lifted her right arm into the air, certifying Agent Broderick as the victor. The audience clanged with applause. Employees rose to their feet for a standing ovation.

"Congratulations, Agent Broderick!" Mr. Mond proclaimed over the sound system. "A huge win for the Department of Vehicle Technology!"

Suddenly, beneath Broderick's feet, the platform opened up and took her down through what looked like an elevator system.

"Director Harlow? Ready for the next round?" Mr. Mond asked.

Viv glanced over at her mom. A spotlight fell over Director Harlow as she pressed a button on her collar, activating the micro microphone sewn into her lapel. Suddenly, her voice, too, was now amplified across the entire arena.

"Excellent, excellent! Well done, Beth!" Director Harlow said. "Anyone else want a turn in the arena?"

"Count me in!" A man's voice rang out from the north end of the complex. The heavy Australian accent could only belong to one man and one man alone.

The searching spotlight illuminated Desmond Frank, Charlotte's dad. His blond hair was endearingly messy, and a stubbly beard surrounded his jagged, toothy smile.

"Wonderful. Anyone feeling lucky today? Do we have a volunteer to challenge twenty-time winner Desmond Frank?" Director Harlow asked. "Anyone *not* from the Weapons Department?"

The arena let out a collective laugh.

"I'll give it a shot. Why not?" Another familiar voice. This time, it was Lieutenant Nicolás Padilla, Elijah's father and Area 51's most decorated fighter pilot. He squeezed his way through the rows of knees, politely nodding at each of his fellow employees as they clapped him on.

"Now this should be interesting," Ray said.

Already, Charlotte and Elijah had locked eyes. Having their dads go toe-to-toe in front of an entire stadium full of co-workers was just as much a contest for them.

"Agents and engineers . . . ," Mr. Mond's voice boomed.

"Ladies and gentlemen . . . Boy, do we have a matchup for you! On the eastern platform, you know him. You love him. It's our beloved head weapons specialist . . . Desmond Frank!"

One section in the stands went particularly berserk. Viv assumed it was the rest of the Weapons Department, cheering on their fearless leader.

"Go get him, Dad!" Charlotte shouted into Director Harlow's lapel, her voice ringing through the space. Her dad gave her a big thumbs-up as he made his way to the lower levels.

"And on the western platform, our challenger and trusty veteran pilot, Lieutenant Nicolás Padilla!"

This time, there were still cheers, but the reaction for Elijah's dad was a little more subdued.

Guess there are fewer military people here than I thought.

"Nicolás, as the challenger, what item are you choosing to bring on the platform?" Director Harlow asked.

With a wry smile, he cleared his throat for a moment and reached inside the inner pocket of his leather bomber jacket.

"This." He pulled out a paper airplane, folded into a simple, triangular wedge.

Gasps and snickering washed over the crowd at the sight of the unassuming choice.

"You're sure?" Director Harlow asked. "I know you're a great pilot, but I'm not sure if you're *that* great."

More laughs erupted from the audience.

"It's all I need," Lieutenant Padilla said with a shrug.

"All right. Have it your way. I hope that leather jacket is waterproof." Director Harlow turned her attention to her longtime friend. "And Desmond? What will you be—"

"Tonight, I'll be using a brand-new invention." If it were anyone but Mr. Frank cutting her off like that, it might be a problem. But Viv's mom had the same soft spot for Charlotte's dad that Viv had for Charlotte.

"Ladies and gentlemen, I present to you . . . echo arrows!"

Mr. Frank stuck out his right hand. Within an instant, someone from his department handed him a bow. The arch was smooth and sleek, made of a shiny, pliable alloy.

"Desmond? That just looks like a bow to me," Director Harlow said with a smile. "Don't you need the actual echo arrows to go with it?"

"Nope."

To Viv, they both seemed at a disadvantage. She watched patiently as the two men were escorted to the elevator shaft below the stands. After a few minutes, each reappeared atop his designated platform.

The horn sounded without warning. Mr. Frank was quick to make the first move, pulling back the string on his bow like a seasoned huntsman. Within a split second, he released his grip, but still no arrow appeared. Instead, it was something much more powerful.

Viv's eyes didn't even have a chance to look for one before a vibrating pulse exploded from the bow's arch. It echoed through the air, almost like a bat's sense of echolocation, expanding and quickening as it shot through the space.

The pulse zoomed through the air—a direct shot at Lieutenant Padilla.

Viv cringed, awaiting the inevitable impact, when in one fluid motion, he sidestepped out of the way.

Viv looked over to Elijah. "Have his reflexes always been that good?"

Elijah nodded. "Ever since I could remember. We've never had a broken glass in our house. He says it's from years of flying planes, but I think he's a mutant."

As Mr. Frank took aim, a familiar face in the crowd across the arena caught Viv's attention. It was Dr. Sabrina Frank, Charlotte's mom. Her deep red hair was so dark, it almost looked purple, and her face sat in a stoic pout. Even with her husband engaged in high-tech combat, nothing could seem to illicit an emotion out of her. Viv often wondered how gregarious and loudmouthed Charlotte could be the daughter of someone so put together.

Mr. Frank let loose a barrage of echo arrows, each homing in more precisely on their target than the last. But none were quicker than Lieutenant Padilla. He dodged each blast with ease before pulling out his paper airplane.

What's he doing? How is that supposed to help?

With a flick of his wrist, Lieutenant Padilla lofted the palm-size plane into the air. For a few gentle moments, it soared peacefully on the breeze of the arena. A rattling noise broke the silence as the tiny paper craft shook violently. Before Viv's eyes, it exploded in unraveling panels and plates, transforming into a life-size fighter jet.

WHOA!

Just as the aircraft unfolded, Lieutenant Padilla pulled out a small control panel from his jacket pocket, complete with a joystick, throttle, and an array of buttons.

The engines roared to life as the plane thundered over the top of the crowd, blowing debris and a spray of water up in its wake, soaking Mr. Frank and his pedestal.

The jet circled high above the crowd, on the ceiling, like a vulture spying prey below. Lieutenant Padilla joggled another switch on the controller, sending the jet into a nosedive directly toward Mr. Frank.

Trying to keep a grip on the bow, Mr. Frank ducked to dodge the massive plane but lost his footing on the wet surface. He slid across the slick platform and plunged into the pool of water below, sending a torrent of splashing blue up toward the ceiling.

"And Desmond goes down!" Mr. Mond exclaimed.

"No!" Charlotte wailed.

"Yes! Woo-hoo!" Elijah howled. "Way to go, Dad!"

Mr. Frank fought his way to the top of the waves and spit out a mouthful of water. A huge smile and a booming laugh quickly followed.

The jet refolded itself into squares and returned to Elijah's dad, landing perfectly in his palm like a loyal paper bird.

Director Harlow lifted her left hand up, sending an eruption of applause and cheers through the sea of onlookers.

"And your clear winner, Lieutenant Nicolás Padilla!"

"Well, that went quicker than expected!" Mr. Mond laughed over the intercom. "What do you think, Director Harlow? Time for one more?"

She considered it for a moment and checked the watch on her wrist. Viv's logical side wanted her mom to say no so they'd have time to retrieve the map before anyone else found it, but the rest of her hoped they'd have the chance to see another awesome showdown.

Finally, Director Harlow nodded.

"I think we can manage one last round!"

The audience cheered her decision. She was like an ancient emperor, calling on her gladiators for another battle.

"Anyone feeling brave enough to follow that?"

Without missing a beat, Joanna's hand shot up into the air.

"Oh," Director Harlow said. "Ladies and gentlemen, our newest Einstein Fellow, Joanna Kim!"

The employees roared with approval.

"You know, we've never had a participant quite so young." Director Harlow deliberated with herself for a moment. "So, for the sake of fairness, I'll only allow it if you find an opponent that's of equal caliber."

Viv's hand never moved faster in her entire life.

"Me. I'll do it!"

CHAPTER
SEVEN

For Viv, choosing which item to bring with her on the platform was a no-brainer.

"My combat suit," Viv said. "Please."

"Oh, so it's *your* combat suit now, is it?" Director Harlow laughed.

Viv looked out across the sea of faces smirking back at her.

"You know what I mean," Viv said, already feeling her cheeks flushing with embarrassment.

Maybe this was a bad idea.

Viv cleared her throat and tried to muster as much confidence as she could fit into the microphone.

"It's what I feel most comfortable using," she said, still shuffling her feet.

"Then the combat suit it is," Director Harlow said, turning to Viv's opponent. "And Joanna? I know you're new, but you're more than welcome to use whatever we've got here."

"That's okay. I don't need anything from your Gadgets

Room, but thank you." Joanna smiled as FuRo wound her way up her arm.

"Ah. I see. Well, all right then," Director Harlow said, nodding.

Wait, what?

Viv looked at her mom with a wrinkled brow. Judging by the resounding gasps and low-pitched muttering, the rest of Area 51's employees seemed to be just as surprised as Viv was.

Mr. Frank had returned to the rows of seats from his losing performance.

"Director Harlow," Mr. Frank said, still toweling himself off. "She can't go up there without anything. That wouldn't be in the spirit of the game, would it?"

Now that I think about it, I actually wouldn't mind that. Let her go up in pajamas for all I care!

"Oh, Desmond. You underestimate her. I'm sure our Einstein Fellow can handle herself." Director Harlow put a reassuring hand on Joanna's shoulder. "Isn't that right, Joanna?"

The wunderkind stood up a little taller, and the two exchanged a knowing grin. Mr. Frank considered her response for a moment and then relented.

"If you say so, boss," he said, plopping down into the seat beside Charlotte. Viv examined Joanna, searching for any hint of uncertainty. She found none.

This doesn't seem fair.

Unless she's just trying to get in my head.

The arena howled with anticipation as the two contenders

were led down a ramp into the lower level of the stadium. Viv and Joanna walked side by side as they passed below the battlefield. Above them, the ceiling was completely made of crystal-clear glass. The mass of water pressed down from above like a weighted blanket.

Whoa!

Had Mr. Frank still been floating up there, Viv would've been able to see every kick of his legs through the sparkling water. Viv felt like she was in a fancy aquarium.

Joanna seemed unimpressed, as if it was nothing special.

They made their way to the elevator bank. Each door was made of sleek titanium.

There, an agent dutifully presented the thing she'd missed most this past week—her purple combat suit. It was the first time she'd been allowed to wear it since the Roswellians got loose. Besides how cool the suit looked, what Viv really had missed was the way it made her feel. There wasn't much use for it in the old copy room, as much as she would've liked to blast the piles of old papers into dust.

As Joanna checked her appearance in the reflection of the elevator door, Viv slipped on the combat suit like second skin. At some point during the past week, Mr. Frank must've fully repaired the damaged arm cannon because the entire thing was polished, shiny, and looking good as new. The metal felt cool to the touch, maybe even a bit heavier than she remembered. Viv wondered how buoyant it would be if it ended up in the water . . .

No, I can't think that way.

I can win. I know I can.

Once Viv was all zipped up, the agent leading them pressed the buttons on each of the lift doors. Just like the passage they had walked through to get there, the elevator shafts were entirely made of glass. Water swirled around the transparent box in a churning, bubbling vortex. Viv felt like she was a dirty mug in a dishwasher.

The agent nodded and motioned for them to enter. Joanna nodded back and took her position.

With one final deep breath, Viv stepped inside her designated lift. The elevator doors closed and, in one fluid motion, shot up effortlessly, ascending through the swelling currents in the blink of an eye.

The arena lights nearly blinded Viv as the doors opened. Mercifully, the platforms were bigger than they seemed from afar.

She took a few cautious steps out, letting the shouts of the crowd propel her forward with every step. Viv squared her feet into the floor, creating imaginary boundaries in her mind that she knew could start shrinking at any second.

Fear rattled through her like a pinball. Whatever bravery had forced her hand up to challenge Joanna now felt like it belonged to an entirely different person. Being thirty feet up in the air didn't help, either.

She wrapped her hand around the trigger inside the arm

cannon, feeling some comfort from the bit of frigid steel. Her palms were sweaty; sweatier even than the time Charlotte had forced her to try skateboarding.

Viv pulled a deep breath in through her nose to calm the thumping in her chest. She gazed across at the opposite platform. Whatever primal fear was consuming Viv seemed to have no effect on Joanna at all.

FuRo climbed down from Joanna's shoulders and nestled into the crook of her elbow. The little robot nuzzled her creator the way Meekee cuddled Ray. It would've been sweet if she didn't realize at that moment what Joanna's true intentions had been this whole time.

That's what she's using. She's using FuRo.

The stage fright suddenly set in. All these people watching.

One of us is ending up in that water.

Viv took a deep breath and squared her shoulders.

And it's not gonna be me.

The starting horn blasted through Viv's ears. Before the sound had stopped reverberating, she'd depressed the trigger in her cannon, feeling the rumbling of the energy blast growing in the lower chambers of her arm.

She aimed down the barrel, hoping to strike first. In the millisecond before the blast could leave the cylinder, Joanna lunged forward, launching FuRo high into the air. The flash of movement was just enough for Viv to miss her shot.

The energy blast rocketed off too far to the left, completely bypassing its target. Viv's eyes darted skyward and tracked the robotic ferret.

"FuRo, *Erethizon dorsatum!*" Joanna called out.

At the apex of the toss, FuRo transformed. The long tail that had wrapped beneath her body retracted and split into a thousand smaller, sharper spines.

She was no longer a ferret. Now the little robot morphed into a sinister porcupine.

What?!

Still soaring through the air, FuRo curled up into a ball and rained down a torrent of razor-sharp metallic needles straight at Viv. They pinged against the shell of her combat suit like rain on a tin roof. A rogue barb flew by on the outskirts, whizzing by Viv's ear. She turned her head instinctually and watched as it sliced through a lock of her hair, sending the curly chunk drifting toward the water below.

My hair! That thing could've killed me!

So much for safety protocols!

With that, it clicked together in Viv's mind. FuRo wasn't built in Area 51; she was made in Joanna's lab. More likely than not, FuRo wasn't designed with the same safety features that the rest of the weapons at the base had built in.

I'm in trouble.

Viv had to act fast. She loaded up another blast in her cannon and trained it on FuRo as the animatronic shape-shifter fell back down toward the platform.

"FuRo! *Falco peregrinus!*" Joanna yelled out.

Without a second wasted, FuRo morphed yet again, this time into a white steel falcon. She extended her new wings and lifted up with a vigorous thrust, narrowly avoiding a collision with Joanna's platform.

Viv's aim wasn't fast enough. The energy blast flew right by FuRo as her avian form completed aerial acrobatics, rolling on the wind like the fighter jet that had just torn through the arena.

FuRo corkscrewed down in precise spirals, swooping by Viv at lightning-fast speeds. Viv suddenly felt like she was caught in a tornado. Wind rushed around her like a violent whirlwind, stinging her eyes. She contracted her limbs and crossed her arms tight across her chest, trying to stay steady in the cyclone. But it was no use.

FuRo's wing tip slammed into her side, knocking Viv off her feet. The arena bellowed in a frenzy.

No! No!

Viv stumbled back up onto her feet. It was the first time she'd looked down the entire match. The platform had started to shrink and was now slimming rapidly.

"FuRo, *Dosidicus gigas!*" Joanna shouted.

Circling high above, FuRo tucked her wings in tight to her body and dropped into a steep dive, heading straight toward the patch of water beside Viv's platform. Viv tried to follow the speeding blur with her eyes, but another high-speed transformation made it nearly impossible.

Where there used to be wings, a mass of four suction-covered arms sprouted out from each side. Her pair of taloned feet morphed into two long tentacles as her next form came into shape.

FuRo had transformed into a squid, now plunging in and out of the water, shooting powerful ink blasts at Viv. Each surge of black ink slammed into her and obscured her vision. Soon enough, she was drenched in the sticky, motor-oil-like substance. Tiny droplets of spray from an impact bounced up into her mouth. It tasted deathly.

Just barely, Viv managed to pull the trigger in her arm cannon. She felt the next energy blast beginning to charge while she pawed at her eyes with her free hand, trying desperately to wipe away the ink for a clean line of vision at her target.

But which target?!

Do I go for Joanna, or do I go for FuRo?!

Before she could choose, her arm cannon made the decision for her. The blast that had been charging sputtered away into purple sparks. Too much ink had seeped into the workings.

No! It's jammed!

FuRo leapt again from the water and shot another devastating blast of ink.

I'm losing! How could I be losing? I beat back literal aliens, and I can't beat one robot?

The ink splattered across the right side of her body with a forceful blow.

This is it.

I'm out of options.

FuRo hurled another splash of ink at her. The platform was too slick with the black ink to stay upright. Viv's foot slipped out from under her, and she hit the deck with a painful thwack. But the sting that now coursed through her side wasn't her biggest problem. She was sliding straight toward the edge.

Her legs went first, then her torso. The employees in the stands jumped to their feet, thundering louder than ever.

Viv's fingers caught the lip of the platform, dangling her thirty feet in the air.

This can't be happening!

One more hit, and I'm toast!

Viv's fingers throbbed, struggling to hold up the weight of the ink-soaked combat suit and her own body within it.

A muted girl's voice cut through the clatter.

"Viv! Viv!" It was Charlotte, wildly waving her arms around like a frantic insect from her row high in the crowd. "Use the stapler! The stapler!"

The stapler?

What is she talking about?

Then, in that moment, the nearly forgotten weight in Viv's pocket seemed to be pulling her down even closer to the water. It was the stapler she had snagged from the copy room.

My powers.

Whether or not Charlotte knew exactly what she was suggesting, the image of Joanna being knocked off by an untraceable green force was instantly satisfying as it ran through Viv's mind.

I could end this battle with one move.

I could take her down if I just used my powers.

No.

No, I can't.

Not with everyone watching.

But it wasn't in her control anymore. The rage of being humiliated in front of the entire compound was too strong to fight. She felt the glow behind her eyes boil up into a scorching heat.

Viv squeezed her head between her arms and pressed her face into the column, frantically praying that no one in the arena could see the freakish green blaze threatening to tear her eyelids open.

But before Viv could move, FuRo delivered one final blow, ejecting another blast of black ink that sent her careening into the water below.

Viv had lost.

CHAPTER EIGHT

Surrounded by a sky of twinkling stars, a full Nevada moon rose above the willow tree swaying outside Viv's bedroom window.

Viv sat in her desk chair, bouncing a rubber ball against her vivid turquoise accent wall, a color she used to love when she was younger but now made her head hurt every time she stared at it too long.

She glanced into the vanity mirror on her desk and ran her fingers through the section of damp hair that was missing a thick lock of curls.

How embarrassing.

Beaten by a ferret.

After she lost the battle at Game Night, Viv had ridden home in the back of Mr. Mond's car with Ray. Her mom had crowned Joanna the champion and then ran back upstairs before Viv was even out of the water, staying behind at the base to finish up some work. But at this hour, she'd be back any minute. The entire drive home with the Monds was quiet and uncomfortable and not just because Viv's clothes were still drenched from the loss.

You'd think with all the high-tech equipment at Area 51, they would've figured out how to make an instant blow dryer.

The worst thing had been that they hadn't managed to go back to the Forbidden Zone before they left, which meant they weren't going to be able to retrieve the map until Monday. Thinking about it just made the pit in Viv's stomach hurt worse.

Below the lamplight, the stapler that had somehow made it all the way from the copy room sat alone on Viv's desk. Now that it was summer, the usual books and homework that piled up were all shoved into her closet. She stared at the lone stapler. It stared back at her like a rude houseguest.

Viv threw the ball against the wall harder this time, chucking it at her framed poster of Rosalind Franklin peering down into a microscope. It ricocheted off the plexiglass frame and zoomed through the room on a collision course straight back into Viv's face.

The ball froze in midair, suddenly bathed in a field of luminous green. Viv clapped her hands over her eyes, feeling the smoldering heat of the powers she had never wanted—the powers she still couldn't seem to control.

No! Stop!

The ball dropped to the ground with a thud and rolled beneath her bed.

Viv pulled her feet up onto the chair and wrapped her arms

around her shins, burying her head into the space between her knees. Muggy tears ran down her face and tickled her nose.

I can never go back there.

A knock rapped gently at the door.

"Viv?"

Director Harlow's voice was low and patient.

Great. Now *she wants to talk.*

Viv wiped the tears off her cheeks and leaned over to look at herself in the mirror. Her eyes softened into their normal state of green, just in the nick of time.

The door squeaked open, threatening to knock off the row of string lights that were hung up above the threshold.

"Viv? You okay in there?"

Her mother softly tiptoed into the room, saw her daughter was still awake, and plopped down onto the edge of her bed. She kicked off her heels with a clatter onto the hardwood floors.

A million things rushed through Viv's mind. This was the first time the two of them had really been alone since the alien attack, and now that she finally had her mom to herself, Viv didn't even know where to start. If she could, she'd flip that lamp around interrogation-style and fire off questions like a police detective. There were so many things she wanted to know.

So many things I need *to know.*

Her mother spoke up before she got the chance.

"Viv? I wanted to talk. See if everything was all right. You seemed a bit—"

"Why would you let me go up there today?"

Her mom's eyes grew wide.

"I don't understand. You volunteered to challenge Joanna."

"Why would you let me go up there if you knew everything that robot could do?" Viv asked.

Viv's mom sighed and sat upright. "Part of me wanted the rest of our employees to see all the incredible things that FuRo was capable of."

"So you agreed to send your daughter up there as a human sacrifice?"

"That's not it at all, sweetie. I was thrilled for you to get a chance to use that combat suit again. I know how powerful it made you feel. And clearly, after last week, you seem very comfortable in it. I thought you'd have a fighting chance against FuRo. I wouldn't have let any of the other interns go up there, that's for sure. But I knew *you'd* be strong enough."

Viv swiveled her chair around and faced the mirror again. The tears were threatening a swift return. Her mom let out another exhale and reached out, placing her hand on Viv's shoulder.

"Listen. Game Night is a friendly competition. It's not supposed to make you feel bad about yourself. Remember when Mr. Frank lost? He was laughing and having a good time. It's just a game, sweetie."

It meant more than that. How can she not see that?

The words stung. Viv bit down on her lip and refused to speak.

"I know this past week hasn't been very fun for anyone. That's why I was hoping that Game Night would be a great way to blow off some steam. Are you at least enjoying the internship?"

Viv couldn't hold it in anymore. Everything that had been warring inside her finally came spilling out in a torrent.

"Come on, Mom," Viv exploded. "Why are you even asking if I like a stupid internship or how I'm feeling after Game Night, when you clearly don't care? You haven't cared enough to tell me the truth for thirteen whole years!"

"What's gotten into you, Viv? What are you talking about? Of course I care a—"

"Megdar told me the truth. I know everything now."

The room stood still for a moment. Only the chirping of the desert crickets filled the space between the two Harlows.

"Is it true?" Viv pressed.

"Is what true?" her mother finally replied, looking faintly shell-shocked.

"Did you steal a sample of his DNA and inject yourself with it?"

The next few moments passed like the ticking of a bomb. Her mom would either come clean and confirm Viv's deepest fears, or—even worse—she would lie, and Viv would spend the next years of her life stuck, impossibly existing in a house that would never accept her for what she was.

"Yes," Cassandra said with resignation. "It's true."

Viv felt her stomach flip over. Of course, it was obvious that Megdar was telling the truth, but to hear the words come out of her own mother's mouth was another story.

"I was young and naive. It was completely reckless. I thought maybe if I could bypass the regulations, get a real concrete example of human and alien genetic transfer, I could get the director's attention," she said, almost embarrassed. "It was stupid of me. Dangerous, too. Regardless, I was wrong. I was extremely lucky that nothing happened."

Viv felt the muscles in her neck tense up.

"What do you mean you were wrong?" Viv asked.

"Something was off. I didn't experience any changes to my genetic structure. Either my calculations were wrong or the entire theory of intermingling Roswellian and human DNA was faulty to begin with." Cassandra sighed. "But it ended up working out for the best."

You're kidding. She really has no idea.

Half of Viv wanted to take it all back, pretend like she hadn't said anything, and never mention it again. The other half wanted to lift that stapler into the air and break it in half before her mom's very eyes.

She should know what she did to me.

She should know that she made her daughter into an alien-human monster.

"But that was so long ago, sweetheart," she said. "Why would he even tell you that?"

Viv could barely contain the edge in her voice. "Because you were pregnant at the time. With me, Mom."

Cassandra's mouth fell open. She caught herself and fixed her expression back to mild curiosity.

"Megdar knew I was pregnant?" She shifted again on the bed. "How is that possible? I didn't even know at that point . . ."

Her words trailed off as if deep in thought, trying to transport herself back to that day. Viv clenched her hands together in her lap.

Here it was. The perfect opportunity to tell her mom. To explain exactly why Megdar knew she had been pregnant that day. To shove in her mom's face just how wrong she had been. To make her feel even one ounce of the fear, uncertainty, and stress that Viv had experienced in the last week. She opened her mouth to let it all out, and then—

"Yet another thing I'm so thankful for," Cassandra said. "When you were born, you were a perfect, healthy baby. There's nothing more in this world that a mother could ask for."

A lump pushed up from the back of Viv's throat. She felt like she might puke, and the hateful words died behind her tongue. She couldn't tell her mom now. Viv could never reveal to her that her "perfect" daughter was actually a monster. Her mom would never look at her the same way again, and she wasn't sure if she could handle that. So instead, she forced deep down all her fears and anger about her alien half.

"You lied to him," Viv said. She still had plenty to be angry with her mom about. "You said that you would free him and the other Roswellians."

"I didn't lie to him, Vivian," Cassandra said. She reserved Viv's full name for when she meant business. "I had every intention of releasing them. And I still would have if they hadn't tried to escape and attack the base. But when I first met Megdar, I was nothing. Just a low-level employee. Nobody at the base was going to listen to my requests. Even when I eventually was promoted to director, it became very clear that not everything at the base is under my control."

"What do you mean? Aren't you the top person in charge now?"

"Viv, Area 51 is part of a much larger network. The work we do affects every single living person on Earth. There are governments around the world that we have to answer to at the end of the day. You wouldn't believe how much trouble I'm in for allowing the Roswellians to escape. That's why I've been working so late recently."

"Really? You're in trouble?"

Her mom tightened her lips into a half smile.

"Big time. The US government trusts me to keep all their secrets safe," she explained. "And when things go wrong, I'm the one who has to take the blame. If the world knew about even half the things Area 51 keeps secret, there would be panic. Chaos."

Viv flashed back to earlier that day in the Forbidden Zone, when she and her friends had discovered an entire underground zoo of mythological creatures hidden just beneath the feet of Area 51's employees.

The werewolves. The swamp creatures. The thunderbird.

That terrifying Chupacabra.

Is Mom the one keeping them locked up? Or is it someone else?

That last thought reminded her of a final question she had for her mom, while they were laying everything out on the table. Or, almost everything.

"Who's Ernest Becker?"

Cassandra pulled her hand away. Her eyes lowered and her brow furrowed as though the name knocked something loose inside her.

"Where on Earth did you hear that name?"

"In the copy room. While we were shredding documents. We found a picture attached to a file, and you were laughing with him," Viv explained.

Her mom closed her eyes. A warm smile spread across her lips, and she leaned back against the wall.

"He was . . . an old friend of mine. Used to work at Area 51 a long time ago. He was one of the first friends I made in the Department of Future Technology," she said, letting out a sigh.

Viv gnawed on her lip. "Just a friend?" she asked her mom. She couldn't help it. Ever since she had seen that photo, a tiny part of her in the back of her head had wondered if, just maybe, the person making her mom laugh that way had been her father.

Her mom paused, then simply said, "A very good friend." Then she cocked her head to one side. "What did you do with the photo? Shred it?"

"No. I think Ray filed it away."

Her mom breathed out another huff and rubbed her forehead with the back of her hand.

"It's been a long day," she said, fluttering the covers on Viv's bed and patting down a spot for her daughter to come sit. "Why don't we talk about this tomorrow?"

Viv had known her mom long enough to know when she was avoiding something. In fact, she'd known her for her entire life.

But as much as she wanted more answers, her mom was right. It had been a long day, and Viv could already feel her eyelids pulling themselves closed like a heavy velvet curtain at the end of a Broadway show. She crossed the room and dragged herself onto the mattress.

"Okay."

Cassandra stood from the bed, switched off the lamplight, and stood in the threshold of the doorway.

"Let's do something fun this weekend. Just the two of us," her mom said.

Viv pulled the comforter up over her shoulders and grunted in agreement. She still hadn't fully forgiven her mom, but she was too tired to argue.

The door softly clicked shut, and Viv was left alone again, with nothing but the moonlight cascading down through her window.

CHAPTER NINE

PING!

   PING!

   PING!

For a split second, Viv thought she was still dreaming. The mysterious trilling sound forced her eyelids open in a fluttering daze.

An alarm? On a Saturday?

She rolled over and pawed for the glasses on her nightstand. After pulling them onto her face, Viv squinted up at the alarm clock.

3:25 a.m.

But the sound wasn't coming from the clock.

What the—? My phone?

Still attached to its charging cord, the phone felt heavy in Viv's tired hands. The home screen blinked to life. Only one new notification. It'd been twenty-two weeks since she'd backed up her data.

That's not it.

Her ears finally adjusted to the waking world as she homed in on the sound coming from across the room.

A few feet away, the wrist communicator from her combat suit vibrated against the cool pinewood of her desk, rattling the knobs on the drawers. She'd never given it back after the alien attack. It stayed in her room as a little token, a souvenir of the chaos she'd endured that day.

There was only one other person who had a direct line to that communicator. She felt her heart thudding in her chest, suddenly feeling more awake than ever.

Elijah?

She pressed the button, and instantly, a frantic projection of visual data popped up from the LED screen. But it wasn't who she expected.

"Viv! Quick, I need your help!"

Charlotte's voice was tinny and high-pitched over the small speakers.

"Char? Huh?" Viv said, pressing her knuckles into her eyes, trying to fight off the sleep that beckoned her back into bed. "What's going on?"

Viv focused on the small image of her best friend. Behind Charlotte's messy blond hair, the background seemed too sleek to be her room. It looked familiar.

Weird. It almost looks like . . .

"Charlotte? Are you at Area 51?" Viv asked.

"There's an emergency! I don't know what happened!" Charlotte said, her voice crackling on the line. "One of the creatures from the Forbidden Zone—it got out!"

"What? Charlotte, calm down!" Viv said. "I don't understand!"

"I need your help! Please! Come quick!"

A crashing sound cut in from Charlotte's end of the communicator. Viv could hardly make out what she was saying.

"What? Charlotte? Can you hear me?"

"Just get here as fast as you can! I gotta go!"

And just like that, the tiny projection of Charlotte dissipated as the communicator flickered off.

Now Viv really felt like she was dreaming.

Darn. I could've used a weekend off.

Whatever was going on at the base, it sounded bad. Charlotte had always been a night owl, but Viv never imagined that she would sneak into the base at this hour. She sighed, knowing what she had to do.

She changed clothes, slipped on her shoes, and shut her bedroom door behind her with a soft click. As she tiptoed past her mom's bedroom door, the low thrum of her sound machine seeping in from below the threshold calmed Viv's nerves. A few more steps down the stairs, and she bounded out the front door. The dry night air stung Viv's eyes as she made her way to her next-door neighbor's house.

Charlotte needs us. She needs all of us.

"Ray! Ray!" Viv called up toward his bedroom window.

The side of the Monds' yard was decorated with small succulents and an array of multicolored gravel. Viv reached down and picked up a pebble, chucking it up at Ray's window with as much force as she could muster.

It ricocheted off the window with a clink, then silence.

No response from Ray.

She threw another rock.

"Ray! Wake up!" Viv shout-whispered, trying her best not to disturb any of the other neighbors.

It's not working.

She felt around in the gravel until her fingers wrapped around an even bigger stone. Viv pulled back her right elbow and lobbed it straight toward Ray's room.

Just as it was about to strike the glass, a sleepy Ray opened his window.

CLUNK!

The rock whacked him right in the forehead.

"OUCH!" Ray cried out.

"Argh! Sorry, Ray!"

"Viv?" he asked, peeking down through the darkness. "What the heck?!"

She was about to apologize again when something more important caught her attention.

"Ray? Where are your clothes?!" Viv asked.

"I sleep naked!" he said.

"Why aren't you ever wearing pants?" Viv asked, shielding her eyes with her forearm. "I'm getting you a set of pajamas for your birthday, you weirdo."

"Well, sorry that I wasn't expecting any company at three in the morning!"

Ray wrestled on a pair of pants and a T-shirt before leaning back over the side of the windowsill. But he wasn't alone. A familiar green shape sat perched up by his neck like a pirate's trusty parrot.

"Meekee!" The little alien ball of fuzz on Ray's shoulder bounced with joy at the sight of his friend Viv.

"You have Meekee with you?" Viv raised her eyebrow. "I thought the deal was you could only keep him if he stayed at the base?"

"Shh! Please don't tell anyone," Ray said. "I've been sneaking him out. He gets lonely at night without someone to cuddle with."

As much as she wanted to debate this more, Viv knew they were running out of time.

"We gotta get to the base. Charlotte said it was an emergency," Viv explained. "We need to go now!"

"But my dad's asleep. No way he'll drive us!"

"We don't need your dad," Viv said with confidence. She pointed her outstretched thumb across her lawn at the driveway.

"What?" Ray said.

Viv looked back over her shoulder. She was pointing at

nothing. Just an empty space where a car would be.

Duh.

She'd completely forgotten that her mom switched the Humvee back to stealth mode every night when she returned home. The entire self-driving vehicle was completely invisible to the naked eye.

"Just come downstairs!" she shouted up toward the window.

After a few moments, Ray and Meekee met Viv around the back door of the Monds' house. Ray had a twisted look on his face.

"What's wrong?" Viv asked.

"You didn't yell at Meekee for being naked." Ray huffed and folded his arms across his chest.

"Ray. Meekee's always naked!"

"I see your point. We should take him shopping soon."

They hopped into the slick leather backseat of the covert Humvee.

"Dang. I wish my dad had a fancy car like this," Ray lamented.

Viv fixed her attention toward the front windshield. She'd never been in one of these without her mom before but figured she could still get it started on her own.

"AVA. Turn on."

The car sat still, as silent as the early-morning solitude.

"AVA? Engines on." Viv tried to harden her voice in an imitation of her mother's. "AVA. Turn on now."

Still nothing.

"How the heck do we get this thing started?" Viv asked.

"Let me try," Ray said. "After we watched Agent Broderick whip O'Malley's butt, I asked your mom all about her and the work they do in Vehicle Technology."

Ray cracked his fingers and typed a sequence into the screen on the steering wheel.

"This should do the trick." He flicked a lever below the center screen, and all at once, the engine hummed to life.

"Yes!" Viv said. "Way to go, Ray!"

I knew bringing him along was a good idea.

"AVA, take us to Area 51," Ray commanded.

"Wait. We should pick up Elijah first," Viv suggested.

"Is he on the way?" Ray asked. "I thought you said it was an emergency?"

"Should only take a minute."

After her defeat in the arena, Viv was itching to prove to Elijah that she wasn't a loser.

And if that means saving Charlotte from a terrifying creature, then that's what I'll do.

AVA invisibly navigated them through the empty streets, getting them to Elijah's house in record time. He came trudging out of his front door, looking just as worn out and weary as Viv had ever seen him. It had taken a few calls on his cell phone to rouse him out of sleep, but there he was, leaning up against the Humvee's driver's side window.

"Guys? What's so important, huh? Did you steal this car?"

Ray filled him in on the urgent call from Charlotte and her warning about the missing creature. Viv watched as his big brown eyes grew wider with every word.

But she never expected what he'd say next.

"We should call Joanna," Elijah said.

Viv clenched her teeth at the sound of her name.

"Joanna? Why would we need Joanna?" Viv asked.

"She was the only one who knew how to wrangle those jackalopes. What if we need her help capturing whatever creature got loose?" Elijah said.

"Yeah, I guess she helped with that," Viv said. "But we can handle it on our own. She's not the one who fought off an army of aliens last week."

Ray shook his head. "Elijah is right, Viv. The more of us, the better."

"Seriously, guys. We don't have time . . . ," Viv pressed.

"Come on, Viv," Elijah said. "She might be the difference between life or death for Charlotte."

Viv slumped back against her seat.

"We don't even know where she lives," she said.

"I bet AVA does," Ray said, turning back to the dashboard.

Viv wanted to kick Ray in the shins. The last thing she needed was for Joanna to swoop in and save the day. But then she sighed.

Ugh. I think they might be right.

As much as she dreaded seeing her new archenemy again, saving her best friend was more important than petty drama.

"Fine," Viv said. "But let's go quickly. If Charlotte gets eaten because we had to stop at Joanna's, I'm blaming you two."

"I'm assuming we don't have time to get Slurpees along the way, then?" Ray asked.

Viv shot Ray a look. "AVA, take us to Joanna Kim's house," she said into the dash.

"Affirmative. Routing to Einstein Fellow Joanna Kim's residence." The automated voice was calm and smooth.

"Wow, I can't believe how well this thing works," Ray said. "Wonder if it would take us all the way to Las Vegas."

"Now rerouting to Las Vegas," AVA said.

"No! AVA, no!" Viv shouted.

The Kim house was as elegant and pristine as Joanna was. Tucked away in the high-end residential section of Groom Lake, the house was in a gated community, though the invisible Humvee had no problems getting past the snoozing security guard meant to be guarding the entrance.

Every lawn was green with well-watered grass, a rare sight in the desert.

They're rich. No doubt about that.

AVA pulled them up right to the curb of the house.

"Here, I'll call her," Elijah said, pulling his phone out of his pocket.

Viv felt a shallow breath catch in her chest. "You have her number?" she asked.

"Yeah. She gave it to me earlier today," he said, pressing the Call button. "She said we should all have one another's numbers, for situations exactly like this."

As much as she wanted to chuck Elijah's phone out the window, Viv composed her expression into one of careful indifference.

It took me years to get his phone number. Even though I've only had a phone for two years.

Within a few minutes, Joanna had slipped out the front door and was making her way through the grass toward the Humvee.

"What are you guys doing here?" she said with a half yawn.

Viv glanced down. Joanna was dressed in green silk pajamas and a pair of dirty sneakers that looked out of place with the rest of the ensemble. It didn't take much to convince her.

She hopped in the backseat, wedging herself right between Viv and Elijah. It took everything in Viv's power not to unbuckle Joanna's seat belt and tell AVA to eject her from the car.

Great. Just when I thought things couldn't get worse.

✹✹✹✹✹

The drive to the compound felt extra long, even as AVA pulled the four kids into the Harlows' typical parking spot. The entire compound was exceptionally quiet.

The four kids marched up to the main pavilion doors. Viv reached for the handle and flung open the door.

She cupped her hand around her mouth to quiet the startled gasp that flew up from her throat.

Standing just behind the door wasn't Charlotte.

It was her mother—Dr. Sabrina Frank.

"Mr. Padilla, Mr. Mond. I'm somewhat unsurprised to see you here." Her voice was as cold and serrated as a steak knife. "But I expected far better from you, Viv. And you as well, Joanna."

Each of the four kids shrunk in stature, trying to appear invisible beneath Dr. Frank's icy glare.

How'd she know we'd be here?

"Imagine you're asleep in bed, and you wake up to an alert that your own daughter has been trespassing in your restricted wing of the facility," Dr. Frank said with a sigh.

"I already told you, I didn't go down there!" Charlotte protested from behind Dr. Frank.

Viv craned her neck to see her best friend plopped into a chair, her arms folded defensively across her chest.

"*Trespassing* is a strong word," Charlotte said. "I was only exploring. I swear! It wasn't me! How would I know the codes?"

"Perhaps with this?"

Dr. Frank reached into Charlotte's backpack and unfolded a large piece of paper so blue, it could only be one thing.

The stolen map. Charlotte must've sneaked back in to get it.

Viv tried to keep her hands from trembling.

We're toast.

"Mom, I swear! I didn't go anywhere near the bottom floors! I was just in the Gadgets Room. I only wanted to play with the duplicator gauntlets again. You have to believe me!"

"Is that so? Well, someone disabled half of the bolt barriers in the Forbidden Zone. If it wasn't you, then maybe you'll have an answer for this, too?"

Dr. Frank summoned a screen from the wall and typed an array of numbers into the Central Brain. A series of security camera streams pulled up onto the floating pane of glass.

The footage was crystal clear. Though the lights had been turned off for the night, the circular hallway in the Forbidden Zone was lit by the red infrared glow from the floor, making everything appear a strange shade of crimson. And there she was. It was Charlotte, looking just as she did now, with her long hair, her skirt, and her gangly limbs typing codes into each of the touch screens along the glass panels. One by one, the hatches on the enclosures released and flung open, allowing a myriad of creatures to crawl out.

"But that's not me!" Charlotte said. "I never went down there!"

"Then I can only imagine one other explanation," Dr. Frank said, slapping the pair of bronze gauntlets onto the table. "Maybe you're not as skilled with these duplicator gauntlets as you thought."

"Even if it was one of my clones—"

"If it *was* one of your clones, then you're absolutely responsible, young lady," Dr. Frank said. "As if having one unruly daughter wasn't enough. Now I've got fifty!"

Elijah chuckled under his breath. Dr. Frank turned on a dime and set her steely eyes on the fighter pilot's son, who went from smiling to trembling in an instant.

"I wouldn't be laughing just yet, Mr. Padilla," Dr. Frank said. "I checked the security footage from this morning, as well. Seems like all five of you had a little extracurricular activity yesterday during lunch."

Viv felt her stomach flop over. Ray broke out into an instant sweat.

"I told them, Dr. Frank!" Ray said. "Do you have audio on that recording? Because you'll hear it! I was telling them that we should go to the buffet the whole time!"

"You have cameras down there?" Elijah asked.

"You don't think we have surveillance footage in our Forbidden Zone?" Dr. Frank scoffed. "What kind of scientists would we be?"

Viv gulped. Apart from the deep trouble she knew they were all in, Viv was even more afraid to ask the next question.

"Dr. Frank? Which creatures escaped?"

The glowing red eyes of the Chupacabra blinked open in her mind. She prayed that thing was still locked away.

"From what these scans are showing," Dr. Frank explained,

"a few of them. But there's one in particular that concerns me. An ancient creature powerful enough to cause severe damage across the compound. Across the entirety of Groom Lake County, if it wanted to. We've had the creature under control through a strict regimen, but who knows how it will react to being released."

Dr. Frank pulled up one more frame of camera footage. The corner of the image read "Terrarium Sector Twenty."

A frozen chill crawled up through Viv's bones. On the screen, a barren stretch of icy tundra extended beyond the view of the camera. Dr. Frank zoomed in on the open hatch and the set of colossal footprints tracking away through the snow.

"The Yeti."

CHAPTER
TEN

Viv's mind ran wild with terrifying imagery. Every book she'd ever read with the Yeti flashed through her brain. A monstrous, apelike beast with dripping fangs and razor-sharp claws stomped across her imagination.

"The Yeti?" The words felt like putty leaving her mouth.

"Yes," Dr. Frank said. "A creature strong enough to snap you in half like a toothpick if it wanted to."

"Whoa," Ray said as he stared at the creature's tracks on the monitor. "That's a biiiiiig foot."

"Yes, and we need to recapture it before the other agents arrive for the day," Dr. Frank added.

"B-but it's a Saturday?" Ray said.

"Saturday or not, Area 51 never sleeps," Dr. Frank said. "In just a few short hours, there will be dozens of people here. It's up to us to get the base back in order before they arrive. You all created this mess, and you'll be the ones to clean it up."

The four interns exchanged a nervous glance. Joanna kept

her eyes on Dr. Frank, not an ounce of apprehension in sight.

"If the escaped creatures are still in the terrarium, we have a chance to contain them before the entire base descends into chaos," Dr. Frank explained.

"Shouldn't we maybe call in some backup?" Ray asked. "Like, I don't know, some experts on these creatures? Maybe we wait until other people get here and try then?"

"I've already got my team on their way," Dr. Frank said. "My hope is to keep this mistake contained as much as possible. If anyone finds out, we'll all be in huge trouble. Myself included."

"So, you're expecting us . . . the five kids . . . to capture the Yeti that can snap us in half like a toothpick?"

"Unless any of you know how to repair damaged Department of Defense–grade WDB247 enclosure doors?"

Every eye in the room looked to Joanna, the most likely candidate. "Don't look at me. I build biologically accurate robots, not holding cells."

"That's what I thought," Dr. Frank said. "So, yes. I expect you five to recapture the loose creatures, starting with the Yeti. And Charlotte, I expect you to get your duplicates under control. The last thing we need is more Franks running around here and causing trouble. Think of this as your chance at redemption."

Thankfully, it seemed like Dr. Frank wasn't going to let them go after the cryptids without some firepower. Viv felt a bit of a thrill to see what Dr. Frank had already retrieved for them from the Gadgets Room. She laid the gear, in all its shimmering glory, out on one of the pavilion tables.

There they were: the orange flight suit. The purple combat suit. The blue growth ray. The bronze duplicator gauntlets. Viv knew her friends had missed the power of these devices as much as she had.

"As for the Yeti, it will be incredibly difficult to find it in the tundra section," Dr. Frank explained. She spun on her heels and focused her gaze on one intern in particular.

"Elijah, that's why I want you to go after it," Dr. Frank said. "With you in the flight suit, I believe we might have a chance to spot it from above."

Viv searched Elijah's face for a hint of fear, but his eyes stayed steady.

"I can do it," he said. "You can count on me, Dr. Frank."

Viv couldn't help but smile.

That attitude is exactly what makes him so special.

"That attitude is exactly why I'm sending Joanna with you," Dr. Frank said. "I need the rest of you here to help me recapture the less dangerous creatures."

Viv's smile immediately dropped.

What?! No!

"Joanna, I assume you're familiar with *Dinanthropoides nivalis*?" Dr. Frank said.

"Yes, of course," Joanna said. "Only in a theoretical context, but yes, I'm familiar with the Yeti."

"Excellent. Luckily, at Area 51, we're only charged with

containing creatures endemic to the Americas. Keep in mind that this particular specimen is a Canadian Yeti. It's typically more docile than its Tibetan counterparts but nearly double in size. I want you to go with Elijah and assist in the recapture."

"Absolutely. I'm more than willing to help," Joanna said. "I also wanted to formally apologize. I feel partly responsible for accompanying the interns down there in the first place."

Viv's spine stiffened at the backhanded lie.

Accompanying us? It was her idea! She's the one who led us down there!

"I appreciate your honesty, Joanna," Dr. Frank said. "But once you and Elijah return, and the Yeti is secured back in its enclosure, we'll discuss a fitting penalty. For all of you."

Perfect. Now Joanna and Elijah get to save the day together. And she has more time to flirt with him.

Elijah cleared his throat. "But after we sneak up on it, then what do we do?"

In response Dr. Frank whipped open one of the drawers on the long titanium desk in front of her.

"Ah. Here we are."

She held up a smooth white button. It fit perfectly in her palm. A gray silhouette of the Yeti was emblazoned on the front. Even on the tiny device, the outline of the creature sent a tingle through Viv's skin.

"These are control buttons," Dr. Frank explained, handing the small button to Elijah. "When they were originally captured, each cryptid was injected with corresponding nanochips. Once the buttons are pushed within the range of the creatures, they'll be subdued into a docile state. After they're asleep, they'll be much easier to relocate back into the Forbidden Zone."

Ray snatched the button out of Elijah's hand and looked it over with curiosity.

"This would've been useful earlier, huh? With the jacka-lopes?" he said.

"Ah, yes. Thanks for reminding me, Ray," Dr. Frank said. "I'll factor in that little incident when I decide on an appropri-ate punishment."

Yet again, Ray's shins were looking particularly kickable.

"How far away do we need to be for the button to work?" Joanna asked.

"Approximately ten yards," Dr. Frank said. "Once you've gotten that close, press the button and the nanochips are pro-grammed to release the perfect chemical cocktail of neuro-transmitters that will put the creature right to sleep."

"To sleep?" Ray said. "Like, a nap?"

"Precisely. I've already started the containment process. The Ozark howlers and the splintercats were rather easy to catch with a simple lure. According to my records, of four cryptids that were released at some point around three this morning, all that's left is the Yeti and the jackalopes."

Just then, the Central Brain's alarm sounded in its distinc-tive high-pitched staccato.

"Great. Now what?" Dr. Frank said, turning back to the broad screen. She plunged her hand into the glowing orb of blue light. It recognized her palm scan and switched to green.

"Show cameras from the northwest region of the Forbidden Zone, enclosures fifteen through thirty."

A new security feed opened on the screen, this time, around the front bend of the circular zoo. The footage looked eerily familiar.

There she was again. Charlotte, bathed in the eerie red light and typing away in the darkness onto yet another enclosure's touch screen. The ceiling enclosure door slammed open with a violent thrust. After a split second, the shadowy beast crouching out of view of the camera slithered up the walls and out of the open ceiling.

"See? I told you it wasn't me!" Charlotte shouted. "I'm right here, and I don't even have the gloves on!"

"No. It can't be," Dr. Frank said breathlessly.

Viv wasn't sure if she'd ever seen Dr. Frank reveal this much emotion. In fact, Viv wasn't convinced Dr. Frank had ever experienced any emotion at all in her life until this moment.

"What is it?" Elijah asked.

"There's only one cryptid more dangerous than the Yeti. And it's just been released," she said. "Now we really must move fast."

"Mom?" Charlotte asked. "Which creature was it?"

Dr. Frank looked down at her hands.

"The Chupacabra."

In that moment, Viv wished she'd stayed home. No matter what kind of trouble Charlotte had managed to create for herself here, none of it was worth going up against something that terrifying. Viv didn't want to imagine getting anywhere close to that thing, let alone ten yards. But before she could say anything—

"Charlotte. Viv. I want you two to head into the terrarium and track down the Chupacabra." Dr. Frank pinpointed the subsector on the Central Brain's map. "Looks like it's in the desert biome. This is a highly dangerous vampiric creature. Many of the legends claim that when provoked, the Chupacabra has been known to use mind control, though we've never seen this power since it's been here at Area 51."

Mind control?

"Are you sure it's safe for us to go after it?" Viv said.

"Do you think I would send in my own daughter if it wasn't safe?" Dr. Frank said. "With these control buttons, it's perfectly safe. No offense, but a child could do it."

"None taken," Ray said.

"We're running out of time," Dr. Frank said. "Clearly, these duplicator gauntlets are malfunctioning. For them to be creating duplicates that don't disappear after a few minutes, there's got to be something really wrong. Charlotte, please be careful with them."

"What about me? What should I do?" Ray asked. "Stay here and cheer you on while you fix the gates?"

Dr. Frank didn't even look up from the screen.

"No. In fact, I have an extra special task for you, Mr. Mond," she said. "There is one cryptid that we don't store in the Forbidden Zone. I'd like you stationed there to watch over it. In case any of these rogue clones choose it as their next target."

"You're sending me somewhere . . . alone?"

"Oh, don't be so frightened," Dr. Frank said. "I doubt the clones would even know where to look. Besides, you're not alone. You have Meekee, don't you?"

"Meekee!" the alien pipped from Ray's shoulder.

"Um, Dr. Frank?" Ray said, scratching at his scalp. "Can I ask which creature it is?"

"Ever heard of the Loch Ness Monster?"

Viv could hear Ray's gulp from across the room.

"I thought you said Area 51 only had creatures from the Americas?" Joanna asked. "Isn't the Loch Ness Monster from Scotland?"

"Indeed, it is. But it's currently on loan to us from MI6."

While Joanna's eyes lit up with fascination, Ray's knees started to wobble.

"Oh, Mr. Mond, pull yourself together. If worse comes to worst, you'll have the growth ray with you."

"W-w-why don't you keep the Loch Ness Monster in the Forbidden Zone?" Ray choked out.

Dr. Frank pinched her eyebrows together as if the answer was painfully obvious.

"Oh, Nessie's much too big to keep down there."

CHAPTER ELEVEN

Even at almost five in the morning, the artificial sunlight that lit the desert sector of the terrarium was glaringly bright. The heat was just as unbearable. Zipped all the way up inside the metal of the combat suit, Viv felt like one of the chicken tenders under the lamps in her middle school's buffet line.

Her suit had thankfully dried out since Game Night in the arena. But now the sand was beginning to seep in through the cracks of her footplates.

She and Charlotte had only been trudging for half an hour or so, and they originally set out tracking a set of gnarled paw prints through the dunes. But the more time they spent out there, the more the wind blew off the curve of the dunes, kicking up granules of sand and covering everything in a gritty mist. The tracks were becoming harder and harder to see.

"What even is a Chupacabra, anyway?" Charlotte mumbled, wiping sweat off her forehead.

But Viv wasn't listening. Her mind was a dozen sectors away, wondering what Elijah and Joanna could've been talking about as they trekked through the icy snow on the hunt for the Yeti.

I bet she's giggling at all of his jokes right now. They're probably having a snowball fight as we speak.

"Viv?" Charlotte said, waving her hand in front of her friend's face. "Hello? Earth to Harlow?"

Viv blinked a few times.

"Sorry, what'd you say?"

"I said I don't even know what we're looking for," Charlotte griped. "What's this Chupacabra supposed to be like?"

"I barely got a glimpse of it this morning, but it was creepy," Viv said. "Look it up on your phone."

"I would if any phones worked here," Charlotte said. "Why do you think I had to call you from Elijah's wrist comm?"

Viv sighed and racked her brain until a few puzzle pieces clicked together, courtesy of a year of middle-school Spanish.

"The verb *chupar* means to suck, and *cabra* means goat."

Charlotte let out a cackle that would've reverberated off the trees in the area, if there was any life at all to be found in the desert.

"You're telling me we've been looking for a 'sucky goat' this whole time?"

"No. I think more like a creature that sucks the blood of goats . . . or people . . . killing them quickly."

Charlotte clammed up. Even Viv felt the fear bubbling as the words came out of her mouth.

A goat was one thing, but a vampire beast that went around killing unsuspecting prey was way, way scarier.

"Okay . . . But I don't know how it could be hiding out here," Charlotte said. "You'd think we'd be able to see it."

Charlotte was right. Growing up in Nevada her entire life, Viv was no stranger to deserts. She'd taken countless road trips and hikes through the trails of the Mojave. But this was something different. There were no cacti, yuccas, or wildflowers to break up the monotony. Just lifeless yellow sand. From their vantage point, she felt like they could see for miles.

Viv began to understand how people could hallucinate all sorts of things out here, especially now that the fatigue of the early morning hour was starting to weigh on her. Each plodding step up the unforgiving sand was becoming more and more of a strain.

The whole reason we're even out here in the first place is because of Charlotte. I'd be in bed right now if she hadn't decided to sneak into the base like a numbskull.

And Elijah wouldn't be alone with Joanna.

"Tell it to me straight," Viv said. "What were you thinking tonight?"

Charlotte kicked at some sand on the ground.

"You didn't actually release all these creatures, right?" Viv pressed.

When Charlotte's eyes finally met Viv's, she almost looked hurt.

"You don't believe me, either?" Charlotte asked.

"I want to believe you, I do! But I saw the footage, Char," Viv said. "It's pretty hard to say you weren't involved at all."

"It was a rogue clone!"

"Last week, you didn't have any problems controlling the duplicates in a battle against a bunch of aliens. But now when you're all alone at the compound in the middle of the night, you can't keep track of them? How does that happen?"

"How should I know?"

"If the gauntlets are just malfunctioning, then why would one of your duplicates release the Yeti?" Viv said. "I still can't understand."

Charlotte scoffed and rolled her eyes.

"You say that as if weirder stuff doesn't happen here all the time," she muttered under her breath. "I should really be the one asking questions."

Viv stopped in her tracks. At this point, the sand was situated well between her toes.

"What do you mean?" Viv asked carefully.

"I think you know exactly what I mean," Charlotte said, her eyes narrowing. "That floating jackalope? Back in the Forbidden Zone? That wasn't because of a magic stapler, was it?"

Viv felt her heart seize up in her chest. Charlotte looked at her dead in the eyes. Viv only had a split second to get her facial expression under control before she gave herself away.

She took a deep breath and folded her arms across her

chest, trying to hide her pounding pulse.

"Charlotte, I honestly have no idea what you're talking about."

"Don't play dumb, Viv. Even my mom saw the footage. She asked me how we caught that jackalope before it sprinted up the stairs. I told her I had no idea, but somehow you did it."

Oh no. Dr. Frank saw, too?

"I'm your friend, Viv! Tell me what really happened back there."

Viv searched her brain for the right words to say.

I'm not ready for this. Charlotte, why couldn't you just believe me before?

"It—it," she said. "It was the stapler?"

"Viv." Charlotte grabbed her by the arm. "I saw your eyes. They were glowing. And trust me, I searched and searched through my dad's blueprints in the Gadgets Room. There wasn't anything in there about a magic levitational stapler that makes your eyes explode with green light. Why do you think I was sneaking around here tonight in the first place? It wasn't just to find the map."

Viv clenched her hands into fists and held them by her sides, trying desperately not to faint. This couldn't be happening.

"Something else is going on," Charlotte said. "I know it. I can feel it in my bones. You've been so quiet this past week. And you almost got abducted by aliens, but you don't seem scared. You seem sad."

I should've known. Charlotte knows me too well.

It's only a matter of time until she pieces it together.

Viv resigned herself to her fate. She sucked in a deep breath.

"I have alien DNA," she whispered.

"What?" Charlotte leaned in closer.

Viv strained her voice low and repeated herself, trying to keep as quiet as possible on the likely chance that they were on some sort of security footage somewhere.

Then, quickly and carefully before she could stop herself, she relayed the major details of the story to her best friend, explaining how her mom injected herself with Megdar's DNA all those years ago and how Viv had no clue until just a week ago. It all came pouring out, and Viv felt an odd sense of relief, mixed in with her terror.

Charlotte was silent for a long moment.

Oh no. She must think I'm a monster. I knew this was a terrible idea.

Viv stared into her friend's bright blue eyes, searching for any sign that she'd just processed the information.

"Charlotte?"

No response.

"You don't have any follow-up questions?" Viv said. Now she was the one waving a hand in front of her friend's face.

"CRIKEY, Viv!" Charlotte nearly jumped on top of her with an explosion of energy. "That's the COOLEST THING I'VE EVER HEARD!"

"Wait, really?" Of all the responses Viv was expecting, this was not one of them.

"Yes! Are you kidding? You're not joking me, right?" Her Australian accent was out in full force now.

"I wish I was kidding," Viv said.

"My best friend is part alien?! AND you have powers?!" Charlotte asked. "What kind of things can you do? Turn yourself invisible? Shape-shift? Ooh! Can you tell what time it is in Australia?"

"I—of course, I can tell what time it is in Australia," Viv replied, shaking her head. "Anybody could!"

"Wow! So cool! What else?"

"Well, as far as I know, just, um . . . telekinesis."

"Pick me up right now!" Charlotte exclaimed.

"What? No!" Viv said. "That's not how it works!"

"Come on! You did it with the jackalope! I'm not that much heavier!"

Viv didn't even find the onslaught of questions annoying, that's how relieved she felt.

"No. It's not like that. I don't have full control over it yet," Viv said, turning her feet and restarting the march ahead. "We can talk about all this stuff later."

"You're like an alien superhero! You're like a Guardian of the Galaxy . . . or Guardian of Nevada. Does this mean that you and Meekee can read each other's minds? Will you end up looking like Megdar when you're older?" Charlotte excitedly asked question after question, practically screaming.

"Shh!" Viv said. "What if your mom is still listening?"

Charlotte ran the gauntlets up through her hair in amazement. "Oh man! I can't wait until Ray and Elijah hear about this!"

"No! No way," Viv said. "You can't tell them anything. You can't ever tell anybody about this."

"Come on! At least let the boys know!" Charlotte said. "Think of all the cool stuff we could do!"

"Charlotte. I'm serious. You have to keep this whole thing a secret."

"Or what? You'll eat me with your creepy alien tentacles?"

Viv's stomach twisted into knots, and she turned away.

"See? This is what I was worried about!" Viv said. "That's why I didn't tell you in the first place."

"Geez! Lighten up! I'm just joking, Viv!" Charlotte laughed.

Viv clammed up. What Charlotte didn't realize is that she'd just touched on Viv's biggest fear . . .

I don't know how I could live with myself if I ever hurt one of my friends . . .

The way I almost hurt Elijah last week.

Her mind raced back to the imagined vision of her crush, walking through the snow with Joanna.

They're out there right now. Together in the cold.

As much as Viv had faith that Elijah would be okay squaring off against a giant monster, she couldn't help but hope the opposite for his companion.

If the Yeti decided to eat Joanna, I would understand.

"I wonder if they're having any luck with their search in the tundra," Viv said.

We need to find this Chupacabra before they find the Yeti. Maybe if we finish early, Dr. Frank will let us go help them in the tundra.

"Let's keep going," Viv said. "We might be getting closer."

Viv took a few more steps forward, and Charlotte excitedly trailed behind, skipping and bouncing through the sand like a flat stone on a calm lake.

"How can you tell? Do you have some kind of weird alien sense?"

"Seriously, that's not funny," Viv said, scanning the ground in front of them. Not a single track was still visible. They were chasing without any direction at all.

"Wait," Charlotte said. "Do you hear that?"

Despite likely damaging it with the volume of her voice alone, Charlotte's sense of hearing was near superhuman. She pointed in the direction from where the sound was coming.

The two girls climbed up a few more steps, reaching the apex of a mound that gave them a better view of the next stretch of desert. A wispy, dragon-shaped cloud floated past the artificial sun, giving Viv just enough reprieve from the blazing light for a glimpse farther along the horizon.

Charlotte was right. There was something out there.

What is that? Is it the Chupacabra?

From their position, all they could see was a blob standing upright.

Whatever this thing is, it's bipedal.

From the brief glimpse she'd gotten of the Chupacabra in the Forbidden Zone earlier that morning, Viv could've sworn that the creature they were looking for would be walking on all fours.

Viv nudged Charlotte in the side with her elbow, silently communicating with her eyes.

We should hide.

The two quietly hustled backward and lay flat on their bellies beneath the dune they'd just climbed up.

Viv peeked her head above the ridge for another glance.

It almost looked like . . .

A human?

CHAPTER TWELVE

Snowflakes fell around Elijah in a dazzling display as he hovered in the air thirty feet above the tundra. He pinched his face together, trying to keep icicles from forming on his cheeks.

There was a layer of conductive metal that lined the inside of his flight suit, keeping a constant flow of warmth streaming through. As well as this system worked, it didn't offer much protection from the freezing cold on his face.

Luckily, Elijah's hair was a bit shaggier than usual, and in this moment, he felt grateful that he'd been too lazy to get a haircut. The extra inch of heat that the near mullet gave brought him some additional comfort.

With the engine on his flight suit buzzing against his back, he surveyed the trail of Yeti tracks laid out before them. The footprints were deep and clear as day. They weaved in and out of the tall evergreen pine trees that scattered the landscape.

We've gotta be getting close.

Wonder how Viv's doing in the desert.

With Ray and Charlotte constantly hovering around in the copy room, he hadn't gotten a chance to talk with her since all the craziness of last week.

That moment on the Roswellian spaceship . . . I wonder if she even remembers . . .

Elijah returned to the ground and wiped some snow off his shoulders.

Before they departed for the VERT Train, Dr. Frank had given Joanna a thermal coat that mimicked the molecular properties of whale blubber. It sat over the top of her pajamas, making her look like a marshmallow with arms.

But even with the high-tech jacket, Elijah could see that her teeth were chattering from the cold.

"Are you warm enough?" Elijah asked.

"Yeah," Joanna said, bringing her shoulders up to her ears.

"I'd offer you my flight suit, but I'm not wearing anything under this."

Joanna laughed, which seemed to warm her a bit.

"I'm doing okay. Mostly just worried that I smell like a whale. Do I?"

"If I knew what a whale smelled like, I'd tell you." Elijah smiled. "But probably."

Joanna grinned back.

Part of Elijah missed the cold. Some of his favorite memories were from when he and his dad used to live in Washington, DC. On winter days when school was canceled, they'd play in the snow, making snowmen and chasing each other around. But that was a long time ago. Since the third grade, Elijah's body had grown accustomed to living in the dry, torrid land of Nevada.

He and Joanna walked past a plot of experiments being worked on by the Area 51 scientists. Vials of mysterious fluids were half buried into the permafrost. Sprouts of unknown crops and plants fought their way through the thick layer of ice that covered everything.

Just then, something exploded out of the snow behind them. Bits of slush flew up and sprayed the two kids.

Elijah almost had a heart attack. He instinctually revved the engines on his flight suit and leapt into the air, lingering a dozen feet up in case he needed to strike down the Yeti mid-attack.

"Sorry! Sorry!" Joanna called up toward him. "It's just FuRo!"

The tiny robot had burrowed its way out of the ground and was now curling up inside Joanna's heavy coat.

The white metal-plated ferret was virtually invisible in the powdery snow. Only her gray face mask differentiated her from the rest of the ground.

Elijah landed back into the snow with a crunch. "You've had FuRo with you the whole time?"

"Yep," Joanna said. "Her batteries were charging at home when you guys came to pick me up, but I figured it's better to bring her on a half charge than not at all. She must have fallen into the snow without me noticing."

FuRo purred against her creator's sternum. Elijah's heart rate was finally returning to normal.

"Can I ask a question?" he said.

"Sure."

"Why is she named FuRo?"

"Well, the scientific name of the domesticated ferret is *Mustela furo*. As a ferret robot, FuRo just seemed right."

As the three continued their trek through the snow, Elijah marveled at the little mechanical wonder. His mind flashed back to the robot's impressive performance in the arena and how it so effortlessly transformed from animal to animal.

That ferret really is incredible.

"So, you're gonna, like, take over Area 51 someday, huh?" Elijah asked.

Joanna let out a melodious giggle and adjusted the hood on her whale jacket.

"Technically, back in California, I'm still a freshman in high school," Joanna said. "I only moved to Groom Lake for the fellowship, and my family's just renting the house for the summer. But my parents think I should drop out of school and take a job in the government. I think they eventually want me to go into politics. Become president or something. All I really want to do is keep working with animals."

"I get that," Elijah said. "My dad really wants me to go to the Air Force Academy High School."

"Do you want to?"

"I mean, yeah, I guess," Elijah said. "Ever since I was a kid, it's been my dream to become a pilot. But the high school is all the way across the country, and—"

"And you'd have to leave your friends?" Joanna said, taking the words right out of his mouth.

"Yeah." Elijah nodded. "Exactly."

He looked down at the snow, partially to see if his toes were still connected to his feet but also to see if they were still on the right path.

Even with the light snowfall coming down, the Yeti tracks were deep enough to be completely visible. Elijah stepped into one, shuddering at the sight of the five huge toe imprints. The big toe alone nearly swallowed up his entire size-eight foot.

"Dang," Elijah said. "This thing must be pretty massive to have feet like this."

"Oh yes," Joanna agreed. "With any Yeti, Bigfoot, or Sasquatch, massive is an understatement. From my research, a fully grown Canadian Yeti could stand up to twenty feet tall."

Elijah shuddered at the thought.

Our ceilings at home aren't even that high.

Elijah opened up his closed fingers and rolled the control button over in his palm, ready to press it the second they were within range of their target.

"You think this little button will actually be able to control such a huge creature?" Elijah asked.

"Let's hope so. From the way Dr. Frank described—"

Before she could finish answering, a massive gust of wind slammed into the two, nearly knocking them both back on their butts.

Elijah couldn't begin to guess how a place like this worked; how each sector seemed to have its own weather system and climate.

But then again, he never would've guessed that he would be spending his Saturday morning chasing down a Yeti.

The wind picked up from the east. From his years of flight training and studying the Beaufort wind force scale, he knew that this particular gale must've been at least thirty-five miles an hour.

And it was getting faster by the second.

Within seconds, the snowflakes that had been drifting on the breeze turned into wads of hard, clumped hail. Elijah felt like he was getting pummeled by a pitching machine.

"What's happening?!" Joanna shouted.

A blizzard.

The two kids were suddenly trapped inside a vortex of violent, whirling winds and whiteout conditions. The sky was filled with so much snow, Elijah could barely see Joanna three feet in front of him.

Trying to fly in this weather would be extremely dangerous. They could get caught on the wind and crash into the frigid ground.

But he had no choice.

If they stayed put, they'd be buried alive.

He extended his wings out, kicked the engine on, and jumped off the ground. In one swift motion, he jackknifed his torso and weaved his arms below both of Joanna's shoulders. FuRo, who had been joyously skittering across the snow just seconds ago, now clung to the hood of Joanna's coat for dear life.

The trio rose up through the squall. Thankfully, the flight suit had a full tank of fuel and carrying their weight wasn't a problem. The issue would be finding a place to land without crashing.

Elijah was determined to get them out of this, even if it meant abandoning the mission and returning to safety. He remembered something his dad always said when faced with flying challenges:

Better to be wise and alive than brave and dead.

A dark spot on the ground stuck out among all the white. Hoping it might be an entrance to a research outpost or the VERT Train that ran through the whole terrarium, Elijah zeroed in on the spot and cut his wings toward it.

Fighting the furious wind wasn't easy, but Elijah used all his might, twisting and turning against every unpredictable blast. He managed to set them down a few feet from the mysterious dark spot.

The three frantically slogged through the snow that was now nearly waist-deep, headed straight toward their potential exit.

But once they got a little closer, Elijah realized what it was.

A cave?

With the wind blowing from the east and the mouth of the cave facing north, a mound of snow was piling up outside the entrance, but the inside seemed to be somewhat well protected.

This might be our only chance to get out of the storm.

Joanna ducked in first, with Elijah a few paces behind.

The winds howled away outside like a pack of hungry wolves, but the comfort from the shelter was immediate. Elijah shook out his hair like a shaggy dog.

"How'd it get so bad, so fast?" Joanna said, brushing globs of snow from her jacket. "Dr. Frank didn't tell us about any blizzards, did she?"

Elijah just stared out into the storm.

Everything's blanketed. That means the tracks will be gone, too.

He sighed.

We failed. We'll never find the Yeti now.

A tap on his shoulder made him spin around on a dime.

"Hey," Joanna said. "You really saved our lives back there. Thank you."

"It's still pretty cold," she continued. "We should find a dry place in here to camp out until the storm blows over."

She motioned deeper into the cave. Elijah tried to steady his breathing. The rush of adrenaline still hadn't died down from their mad dash of a flight.

"FuRo, eyeshine," Joanna commanded.

The little robot had just finished cleaning off the ice lodged in between her metal plates when her eyes lit up with two powerful beams of light, shining like a deer in headlights.

"What's she doing?" Elijah said.

"Well, it's one of the latest features I installed into FuRo. It perfectly replicates the tapetum lucidum layer of tissue in the vertebrate eye system. The same thing that makes dog eyes reflective. It's like having the world's best flashlight, anywhere I go."

Joanna felt around down on the floor and picked up a bundle of pine branches that had blown into the cave, wiped off the snow, and set them down in a small pile on the cave floor.

"Speaking of features, I've been meaning to give this another try, too."

She pointed toward the pile of twigs and gave her command.

"FuRo, ignite."

Now instead of lights, two streams of flames shot out from the ferret's eyes and set fire to the wood.

Whoa!

Elijah jumped backward a few feet.

Glad she didn't use that trick on Viv in the arena!

"It's unfortunate because I can't take her on planes," Joanna said. "But look at us now. I knew that lighter feature would come in handy one day!"

Elijah laughed. "Oh, really? That's the *only* reason you can't take a super-advanced robotic ferret on a plane?"

Joanna smirked and sat down by the fire.

"If I ever have my own plane, you both would be more than welcome," Elijah said.

Another burst of wind raged at the mouth of the cave. Joanna put her hands out over the flames and motioned to the spot next to her for Elijah to take a seat. The fire felt good on his fingers.

"We should try to share as much of our body heat as we can," Joanna said. "It's a common survival strategy among arctic animals. That's why you always see penguins huddled up together on the ice."

To Elijah, the idea of cozying up next to a stranger he'd just met the day before felt a little weird. He looked down at his hands hovering over the fire.

Guess it's better than letting my fingers go completely numb.

Elijah nodded and Joanna leaned into his side. She wrapped them both in the whale coat and the relief was instant. With his flight suit producing heat and the blubbery lining of her coat insulating it, the two were finally warm again.

The sound of a small ping came from down near Elijah's side. It almost sounded like his wrist communicator, but he looked down to see FuRo curled up against his other arm.

For a moment, the warmth of the fire and the steady rhythm of Joanna's breathing calmed him.

If this is how I freeze to death, I guess it's not such a bad way to go out.

A loud bellow echoed from deep within the cave.

Elijah's head snapped up at the sound, low and guttural. Almost like the groan of a gigantic bear.

Joanna gripped him even tighter. They rose from their seated positions and instinctively backed up another few steps, until the corner of the cave pushed back. He felt the untrimmed hairs on the back of his neck stand up. FuRo recoiled and began to hiss at a shadow moving farther into the tunnel.

"FuRo, eyeshine." Joanna's voice shook, but she managed to get the words out.

The ferret's eyes lit up and illuminated a lengthy stretch of rock.

Long, deep claw marks were etched into the wall of the cave.

A few seconds later, FuRo cocked her head to the side as if listening to some sound too soft for Elijah's normal hearing, and her light went out. Elijah watched as the little ferret skittered out of the cave, disappearing into the white of the storm.

Must have a survival-instinct feature built in.

Elijah couldn't blame the mechanical critter for wanting to bolt. From the brief glimpse he got, it seemed like the claw marks ran from the mouth of the cave all the way down, pointing farther into the cavern.

And they looked *fresh*.

CHAPTER
THIRTEEN

Though she'd carefully popped her wrist communicator back into place earlier this morning, now all Viv wanted to do was smash it into a million pieces.

There, on the video projection, were Elijah and Joanna cuddling up close in some dark place next to a small campfire. If Viv had to guess, she'd say that Elijah had accidentally activated his communicator while getting extra friendly with Joanna.

A pain sprang up from deep within her chest.

I knew it.

The jealously fizzed inside of her like a shaken-up can of soda, bubbling and ready to explode at any moment.

Viv slammed the communicator off and dug her wrist into the sand, wishing that the image she saw on it would disappear into the trillions of grains beneath her feet.

How could he?

Short huffs of furious breath came heaving from her nose. She felt her throat closing as salty tears began to sting her eyes.

"Viv?" Charlotte asked. "What's wrong?"

Viv scrunched her face into a scowl and wiped ferociously at her cheeks. She sprang up from her crouched position.

"We should attack that thing before it attacks us," Viv said.

Chupacabra or not. Human or not. Whatever it is, I'm taking it down!

Before giving it a second thought, she let fury be her guide as she took off sprinting down the mound. It was only a matter of time before she could no longer control herself.

Better to get as far away from Charlotte as possible.

"Wait! Viv!" Charlotte called after her.

But Viv paid her no attention. The image of Elijah and Joanna was still seared into her mind, and that's all it took for her Roswellian abilities to come rocketing up to the surface, stronger than ever before.

The burning started from behind her eyes. As if the artificial sun of the desert itself had been implanted into her skull, Viv felt the intensity in a second. Instead of trying to blink it away like she always did, she opened her eyes wider, allowing every ounce of power to flow freely through her body.

The silhouette that she and Charlotte had spotted earlier still stood motionless a few hundred yards away on the horizon.

Anything out here at this hour has to be up to no good. Even if it's not the Chupacabra.

Viv continued her charge, realizing only now that she was no longer running—she was levitating.

Just like Megdar and the other Roswellians, Viv sliced through the air like a knife through butter.

Not even gravity could hold her back anymore.

Her thoughts faded away as she set her sights on the mysterious figure, ready to rain down all her pent-up anger.

She felt like a cheetah, on the hunt for prey, relying solely on instinct and speed to attack.

Her vision blurred as she closed in. With her finger on the trigger, Viv charged up a powerful blast inside her arm cannon.

The figure spun around, now noticing Viv closing in.

"Wait! Stop!"

Her vision rapidly faded back in, the unexpected voice snapping her out of her pursuit. Their gazes met for a moment, and before Viv's mind could wrap around what she was seeing, the man spoke again, this time softer than before.

"Vivian?"

She felt the heat behind her eyes instantly cool at the sound of her own name.

The man's voice was gentle, maybe even a little sorrowful. His posture looked worn and tired. But he was certainly a human and not the dreaded Chupacabra she'd been so eager to pummel.

Her mind came back into focus, too, as the details of the man's face started to register inside her memories.

I must be hallucinating. A trick of the desert heat.

Charlotte finally caught up to Viv. She had her gauntlets poised and ready, with ten Farlotte clones already following behind her. The entire army of blond Aussies halted when they saw that Viv had momentarily paused her attack.

Viv's arm cannon still buzzed by her side, loaded up with the neon purple energy blast that was dying to be released.

How does he know my name?

The man looked so familiar.

"Y-you're . . . ," Viv stuttered.

The face finally aligned with a name, and she realized who she was looking at.

"Ernest Becker?"

The man from the photo from 1999 with her mom and the other agents. She was sure of it now. It had to be him. Though he was a bit grayer in his beard, and he'd traded the sponge curls in his hair for a completely bald look, it was definitely him. But something was off. His form wasn't entirely opaque. His body flickered and glinted in the light—almost like he was a crystal sparkling beneath the desert sun.

The man nodded back at her.

I was right. It is him.

A mass of sickly gray pounded directly into him with lightning speed. The force from the blow sent Ernest Becker careening off the sandy cliff.

It all happened so fast, Viv didn't have time to react. Her eyes followed his flailing body as he plunged down toward the sand below. But her focus quickly shifted to the danger now prowling a few feet away, where it seemed the same fate might be waiting for her and Charlotte, too.

In the light of the desert sun, the Chupacabra was even more grotesque than Viv could have ever imagined.

The creature was completely hairless. Its skin, nearly translucent, was stretched tight over its hunched skeletal frame. If she wanted to, Viv could count every single rib and vertebra. Sharp, bony growths extended up from the creature's spine.

But its face was what really haunted her. A set of large, black, upturned eyes sat above two quivering nostrils, and serrated fangs hung from the corners of its snapping jaws. Inside its mouth, a whiplike forked tongue thrashed in a spiral, seemingly beckoning Viv to come closer. Like when she'd seen the beast earlier in the Forbidden Zone, each lash of its tongue sent flecks of crackling liquid out onto the sand.

Whatever that saliva is made out of, I don't want to know.

With Ernest Becker gone, the monstrous beast set its sights on Viv and Charlotte. It circled them menacingly on all fours, leaving distorted, gnarled paw prints in the sand.

Viv felt beads of sweat roll down her cheeks, mixing with the dried streams of tears that had quickly evaporated in the scorching desert heat.

The Chupacabra reared back on its spindly hind legs, and Viv watched as each fiber of muscle contracted.

It's about to lunge! Should we turn and run?

Her body made the decision for her.

No. It's time to fight.

CHAPTER
FOURTEEN

Ray wanted to pee his pants.

With Meekee perched on his shoulder, he walked through the empty, dark halls of Area 51. He followed the map with directions leading to the home of the dreaded Loch Ness Monster that Dr. Frank had drawn up for him. His every footstep echoed in the vacuous corridors, reminding him just how alone he really was. In his other trembling hand, he held on to the growth ray for dear life, ready to use it at a moment's notice.

Sending us after these creatures? That woman is trying to get us all killed!

Ray tried to conjure up all the information he had ever seen or read about the Loch Ness Monster.

I know it's from Scotland. I like Scottish things. Bagpipes aren't my favorite, but I think I could really look fabulous in a kilt. But kilts can be awful drafty . . .

He thought hard, trying to summon an image of the creature to his mind.

It's got a long neck. It swims really fast. Rows of sharp teeth.

Ray felt his knees begin to wobble. He stopped in his tracks.

"Meekee?" Ray said.

The alien looked back at him with his three big, blinking eyes. His antenna wagged from side to side like a happy puppy's tail.

"Do you know how to swim, Meekee?" Ray asked. "Is there even water on your planet?"

"Meekee!"

"Who? Me? Of course!" Ray nervously chuckled. "Of course I know how to swim!"

He didn't.

"Meekee?" The fuzzy green peach of a creature tilted his head to one side inquisitively.

"Don't look at me like that," Ray said.

Meekee blinked back at Ray, the English words clearly going right over his tiny extraterrestrial head.

"Ya know," Ray said. "I feel like I'm always the one putting effort into this relationship."

"Meekee!"

"Who am I kidding?" Ray said. "I can't swim! I sink!"

He hadn't felt terror like this since at least last week. Ray couldn't remember a time in his life when he'd been so afraid as the moment he'd accidentally shrunk himself in the middle of a battle with real-life aliens. Even the growth ray felt dangerous in his hand. He looked down at the side of the barrel again, checking for the fifteenth time that the knob was set into Shrink mode.

The last thing I need is to make a giant monster even giant-er.

I can't believe she sent me here alone. I do much better in teams.

Meekee let out a squeaking, toothless yawn. Even from an alien, the yawn was contagious, sending Ray into an open-mouthed and laborious inhale.

"I'm tired, too, buddy," Ray said. "Let's get this over and done with, and then we can go back to bed."

He glanced down at the map again. They were getting close. Around a few more corners, and they should arrive at the intersection of the Loch Ness Monster observation area and the Area 51 library.

After another hundred steps, Ray looked up.

We're here.

The iron doors were massive, towering over Ray's head by at least twenty feet.

Drilled into the wall next to the gigantic, bolted latches, a small security touch screen lit up at the motion of Ray's face:

"SECURITY CODE REQUIRED"

Ray looked down at the long, rambling list of numbers on the drawn map in his hands. It was the security code for the door, written out by Dr. Frank herself.

The fear Ray had tried so desperately to stuff down was coming back up to the surface.

"What do you think, Meekee?" Ray asked.

"Meekee!"

"It doesn't sound like a giant monster is on the loose in there, right?"

"Meekee!"

"Who would even have the guts to try and release the Loch Ness Monster, anyway?"

"Meekee?"

"That's exactly what I was thinking."

"Meekee!"

"You're right, buddy. I think we're good to go back. Mission accomplished."

Ray took one last look up at the imposing iron doors and turned to leave.

A sharp burst of static sounded from the touch screen.

"AH!" Ray shouted.

He flipped around in a panic, flailed, and aimed wildly with the growth ray.

Ray felt the zap of electricity leave the muzzle as the security screen was instantly shrunk to the size of a peanut.

Oops!

Though much quieter now, the electrical hum was still emanating from the wall.

"Ray? Come in, Ray."

The voice on the other end was incredibly high-pitched, like a mouse talking into the world's smallest microphone.

"Uh, Dr. Frank?" Ray said. "Is that you?"

She must've dialed in over the PA system. Ray had to hold

back his laughter. It was hysterical to hear her normally stern voice sound so teensy.

"Good. Glad you made it," she said. "Do you have the area secure?"

Ray looked around. The halls were just as empty as before. No sign of any intruders or monsters.

"Um, yes. Yes, I do," Ray said.

The other line went silent for a moment. Ray raised an eyebrow at Meekee, hoping this would be enough for them to head back to the main pavilion.

"Then how are you talking to me from the outside of the observation area?"

Ray gulped and tried to clear the anxious lump that was building up in his throat.

"You can tell?"

"Yes, Ray. I can tell," she said. "I'm watching you on the security footage right now."

"Dr. Frank, please! I really don't wanna go in there!"

"Perhaps you should've thought about that before you and the other interns decided to sneak into the Forbidden Zone."

"But it wasn't my idea!" Ray said. "I never wanted to go down there!"

"You have the control button, don't you?"

"Yes, but—"

"Then you'll be fine."

Ray ran his thumb over the control button and the silhouette of the Loch Ness Monster, sending a shiver down his spine.

"I need to be sure that Nessie is secure. Consider this a requirement of your internship," Dr. Frank said. "You don't want to be the reason we start a war between the United States and Scotland, do you?"

Ray considered it for a moment.

World War Mond.

"No." He sniffled.

"You can do this, Mr. Mond," Dr Frank said. "Believe me. It won't be as bad as you think. I'm trusting you with this, Ray. Don't let me down."

And with that, the itty-bitty speaker cut off.

Ray took a deep breath, switched the knob on his pistol back to Grow, and fired a blast at the security screen. In the blink of an eye, it returned to its normal size.

With Meekee holding up the map for him, Ray typed in the tortuous, drawn-out number sequence.

His finger hovered over the last digit, and as he pressed it down, he covered his eyes with his hand.

The panel sounded out a loud beep as the entrance command was set in motion. Grinding metal and clanging gears destroyed the silence. The doors were opening.

CLICK! CLICK! CLICK!

Ray held the control button out in front of him, frantically pressing it over and over again, in case the Loch Ness Monster was waiting with open jaws on the other side of the door.

This is it.

Being alive was nice while it lasted.

CLICK! CLICK! CLICK! CLICK! CLICK!

Ray still couldn't peel his hand away from his eyes the entire time the colossal slabs of iron were moving. After a while, the sound stopped.

CLICK! CLICK! CLICK! CLICK! CLICK! CLICK! CLICK! CLICK! CLICK! CLICK!

Am I dead yet?

"Meekee!"

Oh good. Meekee made it to heaven with me.

Ray peeked out of an opening between his fingers.

It wasn't heaven.

He was now standing in an enormous empty room, almost like an abandoned warehouse.

"Meekee?" the alien pipped.

"Shh!" Ray nudged him.

The room wasn't completely empty. He tried squinting, hoping to get a better look at the object that sat upright in the middle of the space.

That doesn't look like the Loch Ness Monster to me.

Ray exhaled onto his glasses and tried to rub away the condensation as quickly as he could, but it was still no use. He had to get closer.

Gingerly, he took a few dozen steps farther into the room, with his growth ray out and his finger positioned on the trigger.

It felt like walking through a deserted plane hangar. Finally, he could just barely make out the mysterious shape in front of him.

On a concrete pedestal, what appeared to be a tiny globular glass fishbowl sat beneath a set of bright fluorescent spotlights.

Ray got a little closer. He stood on his tiptoes, trying to see what was inside.

There, swimming around in the water, was the Loch Ness Monster.

It was the size of a goldfish.

"Ha!" Ray couldn't help but chuckle. "Dr. Frank, you joker!"

She tricked me!

"'Too big to keep in the Forbidden Zone.' Yeah, right!" Ray laughed, elbowing toward Meekee.

"Meekee!" The alien jumped for joy.

Ray flicked the edge of the glass bowl, and it rang out with a resonant chime.

"You're not so scary, are ya, little buddy?" Ray said. "I guess they really zoom in on all those photos, huh?"

Teeny-tiny Nessie looked just like he'd imagined it—a long-necked plesiosaur covered in dark green, brownish skin with tapered flippers and a sturdy tail. It swam away from where Ray's finger made contact.

"Suppose I won't be needing this after all," he said, tucking the control button into his pocket.

A sigh of relief calmed his pounding heartbeat. He leaned down and further inspected the legendary beast.

"No need to be shy!" he said. "People make fun of me for being short, too. I just say I'm fun size."

The sound of footsteps from across the room had Ray immediately back on his toes.

He squinted through the empty space, recognizing the shape of the long limbs and the long hair straightaway.

It was Charlotte.

"Charlotte?" Ray said. "I thought you were supposed to be in the desert with Viv?"

He got no response. Instead, she just kept walking, approaching the security control panel on the inside of the room.

"Charlotte?" Ray shouted. "What are you doing?"

Ray peered even harder, trying to absorb her appearance and make sure it really was her.

Something wasn't right.

Her bright blond hair seemed somehow even lighter. Almost white . . . And her skin was the same color. Her entire body had an almost ghostly glow about it.

Oh crud. It's not her.

It's a rogue clone!

The Charlotte clone reached up to the control panel and flicked open the glass covering with a slam.

"No! Stop!" Ray shouted. "What are you doing?!"

Meekee growled and the little hairs on his back stood up.

The fake Charlotte typed in a numbered code, and suddenly the iron doors began to close.

Earsplitting creaking sounds came from every direction. Ray's eyes darted around the room, trying to pinpoint the origin of the sound, but it was coming from everywhere.

Huge metal grates above him slid open, and within seconds a flood of water came pouring in from every corner of the ceiling.

Please, no!

It was as if the room had been turned into one mega bathtub and the faucet was hundreds of powerful waterfalls. Ray was instantaneously knocked off his feet. The waves were raucous and rough, filling the room in a matter of moments.

He fought and gurgled as the water rushed into his mouth. It tasted like a dirty pond, filled with grimy silt and sand. For a split second, Ray felt like he was back in the sewage tubes.

The water overtook the pedestal, briefly sending the fishbowl floating away on top of the current. While he paddled in a frenzy, Ray watched the bowl tip over, spilling out the tiny creature inside.

The second the creature's flippers made contact with the new body of water, the creature rapidly began to expand, causing the glass of the fishbowl to instantly shatter. The Loch Ness Monster stretched out its neck, now at least twenty feet long, and dove out of view.

It's not small! It's not small!

I change my mind! I don't want anything from Scotland!

It reminded Ray of the expandable water toys his dad used to get him for Christmas. He used to leave the miniature animal-shaped sponges in the sink overnight and wake up to a full-size toy.

But this wasn't a sponge he could just squeeze and shrink again. This was a monster, now the size of almost three school buses in length. Its shadow swam below him as he kicked to stay above the waterline, gasping for air.

Ray's glasses had been ripped off his face the second he made impact with the water. He felt around on his face, praying they had somehow gotten caught behind his ears, but they had disappeared. The growth ray was next. It slipped out of his hands and floated just beyond his grasp. He pawed at it, but it was gone, pulled down into the depths.

As the false Charlotte dashed out of the room through the sliver of space between the metal doors, just before they closed shut, Ray and Meekee held their breath as they were sucked beneath the waves.

CHAPTER FIFTEEN

We might've made a mistake coming in here.

With the blizzard still raging outside, Elijah and Joanna had unknowingly trapped themselves in a frozen cave with a monster, and the claw marks on the wall looked like they could've been made by a machete.

Elijah backed away slowly as the grumbling from deep within the rocks grew louder. He put a protective arm out in front of Joanna.

In that moment, a gust of wind from the cave mouth blew in and sputtered out the fire in a single puff, darkening the space once more.

He glanced toward the roof of the cave. The ceiling was low.

Too low to use the flight suit. But if it came down to it, I could use the wings as a battering ram against the beast.

Elijah wouldn't go down without a fight. He wouldn't stop fighting until he was in the Yeti's stomach. And even then, he still might try.

There was the growl again, closer now.

Elijah felt the pebbles on the ground begin to shake against his feet. After a few more seconds, the entire cave rumbled. He extended the wings on his suit, motioned for Joanna to get behind him, and braced for the worst.

The light reflecting from the snow outside only reached a few yards into the cave. But once Elijah could see what was coming, he wished it was pitch-black.

It was the Yeti, barreling toward them at an alarming speed. It was enormous, charging ahead with a fifteen-foot-tall muscular body. Blue hands, blue feet, and a blue face were surrounded by thick, fluffy white fur all over the rest of its body that bounced with every pounding step. Canine teeth the size of dinner knives hung out over the edge of its mouth, and a long, flowing mane of white hair flowed uninterruptedly into a bushy white beard.

It looked like a giant, hairy white gorilla. But a giant, hairy white gorilla with razor-sharp fangs and claws.

The Yeti reached them in a matter of seconds. Before Elijah could react, the beast grabbed Joanna with both hands and lifted her into the air.

The Yeti opened its mouth wide as Joanna let out an ear-piercing scream. Elijah was a millisecond away from pressing the control button before—

"Thank goodness!"

The Yeti spoke.

It—it talks?!

The voice was deep but humanoid. The Yeti recoiled from Joanna's shriek and gently placed her back down.

"Sorry! Didn't mean to startle you!" the Yeti said, putting its gargantuan hands up defensively. "I'm just a big-time hugger."

Joanna had stopped screaming and was now staring up at the creature in pure awe, her jaw hanging open. Elijah took a cautious step forward, keeping his thumb over top of the control button in case things turned sour.

He cleared his throat and hid the button behind his back. "You can talk?"

The Yeti gave a friendly nod.

"Of course! Humans and apes share ninety-nine percent of their DNA, eh?" it said. "You didn't know there were other talking primates?"

Joanna smacked her lips in bewilderment. "Up until this point? No!"

She instantly pulled a small notebook and a pencil from the pocket of her pajamas. Elijah couldn't believe his eyes.

Is she insane? She's taking notes *right now?*

He still wasn't sure they were out of danger quite yet.

"You mean . . . you're friendly?" he asked, still ready to strike if this all turned out to be an act.

"Friendly, eh? I'm a born-and-bred Canadian," the Yeti replied. "Doesn't get much friendlier than that."

"Then what was all that growling and moaning a second ago?" Elijah said.

"Oh, sorry about that. I can get a bit groggy waking up from a nap, ya know?" the Yeti said. "I thought for a second you might be one of those spooky creatures from the other enclosures, so I was getting ready for a kerfuffle. Boy, was I relieved when I saw you two."

"A ker-what?" Elijah asked.

"A kerfuffle, eh? A fight?" the Yeti said.

Elijah and Joanna exchanged a puzzled glance.

Not sure if it's the Yeti or the Canadian part of him that I'm having trouble understanding.

The behemoth crouched and came within inches of their faces. Elijah squeezed the control button tightly in his hand, just in case the Yeti decided to open its jaws and swallow them whole. He couldn't help but stare at the razor-sharp fangs that framed either side of its toothy grin.

Its breath smelled surprisingly sweet.

Almost like . . . coffee?

"Ya know, you two look pretty small to be scientists," the Yeti said. "Are you some kind of different variety of human, eh?"

"No," Elijah said. "We're children. We work here as interns at the base."

"Actually, I'm an Einstein Fellow," Joanna corrected.

"Wow," the Yeti said, standing back upright. Its head nearly brushed the cave's ceiling. "I'm a big-time Einstein fan, too. Hugs and Einstein, that's me in a nutshell. My mom always wanted me to be a scientist. But hey, living here is close enough for me!"

Joanna tucked the pencil beneath her armpit and stuck her hand out for a shake.

"Nice to meet you," she said. "I'm Joanna Kim. What's your name?"

"My name?" The Yeti scratched at its tangled beard with a massive blue hand. "I've never really had a name. Kinda strange, eh? Most folks just see me, shout, and run away."

Elijah's mouth curled into a sympathetic frown. He'd never considered what it would be like to be a giant, sentient ape beast before.

"I met a beaver once whose name was Roger," the Yeti continued. "I really liked that name. Roger."

"I'd be happy to call you that," Joanna said with a smile. She jotted the name down in her notebook.

"Mighty cold out there, eh?" Roger said, motioning outward toward the tundra. "I was born north of Ontario. And when I say north, I mean way up north. Ever been, eh?"

Elijah shook his head no.

"Well, don't go. It's just like that out there. Awful."

"I've been to Canada once. It was lovely," Joanna said.

"Don't get me wrong, the country has its nice spots. I miss the northern lights. Beauty. But the rest of it, not for me."

"But you're a Yeti?" Joanna asked. "Shouldn't you love the cold? Aren't you lonely here, locked up by yourself? What about the others?"

"Others?" Roger said. "Oh, there aren't any other Yetis in

Canada. Just me, since my poor mum wanted to try out skiing for her six-hundredth birthday. I've got a few cousins who live out in the Himalayas, but I don't hear much from 'em."

Joanna tried to keep up with the story, frantically scribbling down every tidbit of information in her notebook.

"May I ask?" Joanna said. "How old are you? Approximately?"

"Me?" Roger said. "Oh, I'm just a baby. I might've lost track of time since I've been living here, but if I had to guess, roughly I'd say two hundred and three?"

"And what does your diet mainly consist of?"

Roger took a second to think about it, then peered down at them both from its jutting brow bone.

"Mostly small American children. Delicious."

Joanna dropped her pencil. Elijah revved the jetpack on his back.

"Oh, I'm just pulling your leg!" Roger said with a laugh. "Sorry! It's been a long time since I've seen anyone. I forget what kind of humor passes down here in the south. Any more questions?"

Joanna was still speechless. She shook her head no and tucked the notebook back into her pajama pocket.

"Not to be a bother, but I'd love it if you could help get me back," Roger the Yeti said. "That is why you're here, eh? To take me back?"

"Take you back?" Elijah said. "Back underground?"

"Yes, of course. Back to my enclosure."

"Wait a second," Joanna said. "You actually want to be back in the Forbidden Zone?"

"Oh yes. Absolutely," Roger said. "When the hatch opened up this morning, I was worried something was wrong. They never open that hatch for me. I thought maybe the power had gone out or somebody broke in. Criminals are so brazen these days. I wandered out to check, but when I tried to get back inside, the latch had already closed behind me. So I made my way to this cave here and lay down for a nap."

"You're saying that the scientists here didn't capture you against your will?" Joanna asked.

"Capture me?" Roger let out an echoing belly laugh. The outburst shook off some of the icicles on the mouth of cave. They came crashing down and shattered against the rocky floor.

"Sorry!" Roger said. "No, they didn't capture me. I was grateful for a chance to get out of the cold, eh? They treat me great here. I wake up every morning to a piping-hot double double from Timmies, no mounties out on Hanoverians poking me with their flagpoles, and I've got my own washroom! I've never been to Hawaii, but I imagine this is pretty darn close."

Elijah and Joanna stared on and nodded with polite, awkward smiles.

The whistling wind outside the cave started to die down. The storm was finally passing.

Roger took notice, too.

"Better get going if you want to be out of here before the

next one hits," Roger explained. "They have these storms up here set on a thirty-minute schedule."

"Roger's right," Elijah said. "We should get going."

Joanna nodded in agreement, and the two kids turned toward the entrance of the cave.

"Do you know the way back to your hatch?" Joanna asked. "Think you could get us to where the VERT Train is?"

"Sure, I know the general direction we need to go in, and I have excellent vision in snowy weather, so it shouldn't be a problem," Roger said.

The Yeti held up one of its hulking hands. Its knuckles were the size of softballs.

"If you give us a ride back to the compound, we can help you find a way to get back into your enclosure," Elijah bargained.

Roger's bright blue eyes lit up.

"Then what are we waiting for?" Roger said. "Pitter patter!"

The Yeti knelt on one knee, hitting the cave floor with a hefty thud. Joanna wasted no time. She grabbed a few fistfuls of white hair and climbed aboard, taking her seat on top of Roger's left shoulder.

Joanna extended her hand. Elijah grabbed hold, pulled himself up, and took his place atop the Yeti's back as they rode out into the icy tundra.

CHAPTER SIXTEEN

Ray paddled as best as he could, trying to keep his head above the waterline as the room sloshed all around him. The flood rose a few feet every second, and the sound of the pummeling torrents raining down from the ceiling was deafening.

The entire hangar was nearly full.

I'm running out of space to breathe!

He could barely see as he tumbled around in the white water. But the shadowy silhouette below was big enough to stick out clearly in the murkiness. Ray peered down between his wildly kicking feet.

It was the Loch Ness Monster, circling beneath the waves like a hunter closing in on its prey.

This time, Ray did pee his pants a little.

He tilted his head back and tried to get a good look at the rapidly approaching ceiling.

The grates above had slatted openings, but the rushing force of the water was too strong for Ray to establish a grip.

He reached up, but his hands were instantly batted away by the pounding deluge.

By this point, Ray and Meekee were completely submerged. Ray opened his mouth to scream, but only a stream of muffled bubbles came flying out.

Bad idea! Can't waste air!

Ray's mind flashed back to a week ago, the moment his shrunken body had plunged into the drainage bucket in his dad's janitorial closet. He'd made it out then. But this time, there was nothing to grab on to—no plastic edge he could use to hoist himself up. Just endless, swirling water.

Beside him, a green figure churned in big circles within the top layer of the water. Meekee had inflated to the size of a beach ball with the amount of air he took in. His three eyes were shut tight as he struggled to stay afloat.

With the control button lost to the waves and the levels rising with no end in sight, Ray closed his eyes and prepared to drown or, worse, be devoured by the Scottish aquatic beast hunting him from below.

Goodbye, cruel world!

Goodbye, Meekee!

Goodbye, Dad!

With his eyes still shut and his lungs burning, he couldn't hold on any longer. He gasped and felt something fill his lungs.

But it wasn't water.

It was . . .

Air?

Ray opened his eyes to a nearly blinding green glow illuminating the water.

It was Meekee. The little alien radiated a brilliant, glimmering blaze of emerald.

What?!

Ray could barely wrap his mind around it.

Meekee has powers?!

The baby alien that he'd been taking home every night, the same little creature that slept by his head on his pillow, actually had super-alien powers.

Within the aura of Meekee's light, the alien had miraculously created two small force fields of oxygen that encapsulated their two heads like scuba helmets.

Ray took a feverish gasp of air, his lungs greedily accepting the oxygen.

"Meekee?! You're a genius!"

Meekee's eyes lit up with joy. Ray wondered why he had assumed Meekee was nothing but a spaceship key.

I guess it makes sense.

He is from the Roswellians' planet.

With the little dome of oxygen protecting his eyes, like a set of goggles, Ray was able to see a bit better through the water. Meekee had bought them some extra time, and Ray was going to use every second. He glanced up, desperate to find any hope of salvation.

There!

On the ceiling, a small rectangular grate of reflective silver shimmered. Having spent a good chunk of the day in the Area 51 cooling system when the Roswellians had escaped, Ray could recognize the color of the cool titanium in a second flat.

An air vent!

We have a chance!

Ray peered down again, trying to locate the beast in the water below. There it was, moving in from across the room, the massive shadow growing larger and faster. The Loch Ness Monster was set on a collision course.

Oh crud! It's coming straight toward us!

Ray waved at Meekee and frantically pointed toward the air vent on the ceiling, begging for the message to get through.

"Up! Up, Meekee! Up!" Ray shouted.

The little alien blinked his eyes, strained, and made a grunting sound Ray had never heard before. More green light exploded out of his body.

The bubble of oxygen pulled Ray straight up by the head. His useless limbs flailed beneath him as they rose toward the ceiling. He felt like a little Chihuahua on Meekee's telekinetic leash.

The tiny alien navigated them up through the water as the Loch Ness Monster picked up speed below.

Meekee managed to pull them up toward the waterline. His grunts of effort were growing louder.

Suddenly, a stream of water busted into Ray's bubble, now

filling up his force-field helmet as if it was a fishbowl and Ray was the fish.

The green light from Meekee's eyes was beginning to fade and flicker.

Oh no. Meekee can't hold it much longer!

But we're almost there! Come on, buddy!

"You got this, Meekee!" Ray shouted. "A little farther!"

They were only a few inches away from the ceiling when the Loch Ness Monster closed in. It swam up at a ninety-degree angle and opened its wide jaws, ready to swallow them whole.

Ray cupped Meekee into his chest and shot his left hand up, mustering all the strength he had left. He wrapped his hands around the bolt of the air vent and flung it open.

Water rushed around them, but with Meekee still doing his best to hold him up, Ray was able to give the final push they needed to pull themselves up to safety. Ray yanked his legs up into the vent just in the nick of time.

The snapping jaws of the Loch Ness Monster missed his feet by an inch.

Ray's clothes were drenched, his glasses were gone, and there was a ten-ton monster still actively trying to eat them, but he and Meekee were alive.

Meekee was exhausted. He collapsed into Ray's hands, his little pink tongue hanging out his mouth.

"Oh no!" Ray said. "Meekee? Meekee, can you hear me?"

Does he need CPR?

How do you do CPR on an alien?!

Ray had only seen people do it in movies. He pressed his lips down onto Meekee face but underestimated just how big his face was compared to Meekee's.

For a second, he had Meekee's entire head in his mouth. He carefully spit out his little friend's face.

This isn't gonna work.

"Come on, Meekee! Breathe!"

Ray crossed the tips of his two pointer fingers together and laid them on Meekee's chest. He paused for a moment before pressing down.

Does Meekee have lungs? Or a little alien spleen? What if I rupture his little alien spleen?

Before he could decide whether to press down, Meekee coughed up a thimble's worth of water.

"Meekee! You're alive!"

He scooped up his tiny friend from the steel vent floor and wrapped him in a tight hug against his chest.

"You're a hero, Meekee!"

Ray couldn't stop the tears from coming. They poured down his face as the alien's eyes blinked open slowly.

"Meekee," he squeaked out with a sleepy purr.

The columns of water pouring out of the ceiling finally started to let up. They went from roaring waterfalls to rain gutters to the drip of a leaky faucet. Ray looked down between his feet at the room below.

Wow. Looks more like an ocean.

The entire space was filled to the brim. The water stopped just a few inches below where the air vents were bolted into the ceiling.

The long neck of the monster whipped back up out of the water, its jaws snapping over and over at the space where Ray and Meekee had disappeared into the ceiling, unable to catch its prey.

Ray crab walked back on his hands and butt, but the Loch Ness Monster's head was too big to fit inside the small vent opening. They were safe.

"Hah! Nice try, Nessie!" Ray said. "I was never worried!"

The sea beast let out a grumbling growl before ducking back below the surface of the water.

Ray banged on the top of the duct, praying that somehow, somebody could hear him from all the way inside the ceiling.

"Dr. Frank!" he shouted. "Dr. Frank! I was wrong! We don't have the area secured!"

He scanned along the ceiling on the off chance that there was an intercom system up here. But everything just looked like smooth titanium.

Of course there's not. Who would want to listen to an air duct all day?

"Dr. Frank?" Ray tried again. "Please! Somebody! We need help down here!"

He got no response. Instead, his ears picked up on another

sound coming from the opposite end of the room.

Not wanting to peek his head out from the vent in case Nessie tried another leaping sneak attack, he craned his neck over the opening at an angle and pinpointed where the noise was coming from.

The colossal iron doors where he'd entered were starting to move. They slowly split open, allowing the water inside to come pouring out into the corridor. With every inch that the gates opened farther, more and more of the tidal wave spilled out.

Ray and Meekee watched from above as the Loch Ness Monster swam out of its holding room, riding a torrent of uncontrollable water into the compound itself.

They shared a worried glance. Simultaneously, Ray and his little friend swallowed down two big globs of nervous spit.

Nessie was free.

"Uh-oh. That's not good."

CHAPTER
SEVENTEEN

Viv dug her feet into the sand and prepared for the Chupacabra to make a move. The grotesque beast circled around her and Charlotte, arching its back and raising its bony hackles into the air. It reared up, letting out a sickening howl—a sound so snarling and inhuman that it made Viv's stomach shrivel.

With one hammering sneak attack, the creature had sent the mysterious man who looked an awful lot like Ernest Becker hurtling off the edge of the sandy bluff.

But Viv was determined to stand her ground. A thundering fury of power grew behind her eyes.

First I have to see Elijah and Joanna together.

Then poor Ernest Becker gets knocked off a cliff.

And now this thing has the nerve to attack us?

Like cracks of lightning over the ocean, Viv felt the electricity surge through every atom of her body. She held her arm cannon trained on the Chupacabra, ready to obliterate her target. Its tongue flicked ferociously behind a row of jagged fangs.

Before Viv could make a move, her best friend jumped in. Charlotte thrust her arms forward, sending her pack of clones descending onto the Chupacabra's position. They formed a protective wall around Viv and the real Charlotte, each with their eyes trained on the creature, ready to pounce.

The Chupacabra hissed, opened its jaws, and flicked its tongue like a whip out across the layer of clones, lashing each with a spray of saliva.

Steam rose into the dry desert air from every point of contact. Each of the Farlottes sizzled and dissolved in an instant.

What kind of acid is that?

The saliva burned so hot that, even in the desert heat, the sand where the clones had been standing caught fire and blazed bright like the embers at the bottom of a fireplace. A few moments later, the granules of sand cooled and crystallized into glass.

Suddenly, the harsh desert light reflected off the newly mirrored ground and into Viv's eyes, forcing her to squint.

With a clear line of sight back on its two targets, the Chupacabra's black eyes turned a bright cherry red, smoldering against the dull, lifeless skin that covered its spindly body. It crouched and scuttled wildly along the sand, growling at the two girls who dared to challenge it.

The Chupacabra reared up, about to unleash a storm of poisonous saliva toward them. Within milliseconds, Viv's instincts kicked in, and her eyes lit up with a dazzling green glow.

She moved as fast as the surge of power through her veins, aimed her arm cannon down toward the hardened sand in front of them, and released the energy blast.

The glass shattered into thousands of tiny shards. Viv wrapped up each fragment in her field of green light and lifted them into the air, reveling in the sudden feeling of control. They sparkled in the sunlight for a blink of an eye before Viv shuffled the layer of newly crushed pieces and formed a protective glass dome around them.

The saliva crashed down onto the dome and melted the outer glass shell into a river of piping-hot magma the color of sweet honey.

The Chupacabra shrieked with rage and let loose another barrage of fiery poison, this time pinpointing one specific spot in the dripping molten glass—the spot directly in line with Viv's face.

It's trying to break through!

Viv's eyes glowed bright green in retaliation. The overwhelming anger sharpened her vision and activated each and every one of her senses.

Crouched beside her, trying to keep her hair from burning up in the inferno, Charlotte tried to summon clone after clone, but each was promptly vaporized the second it came into contact with whatever ghastly substance made up the Chupacabra's spit.

"VIV!" she shouted. "HIT THE BUTTON!"

But Charlotte's voice was drowned out in Viv's ears. The

Roswellian abilities overwhelmed her every sense. Instead of Charlotte's pleas, she heard echoing in her eardrums sounds that she'd never heard before: pulsing waves of pounding vibrations, as if her own heartbeat was connected to the stars of a far-off galaxy.

Her powers were reaching a critical point.

Unable to break through Viv's protective barrier, the Chupacabra flew into a rage. The beast let out a barking huff and began to buck around like a frustrated, wild stallion.

It tried again, this time crossing its tongue like a swordsman, marking a singeing X into the glass shield.

Viv felt the heat of the saliva through her outstretched hands. A singular drop managed to break through the glass defense. It dripped down onto her leg. The tiny bead of poison left a smoking trail in its wake, burning through the purple steel of her combat suit.

Viv shattered another film of glass on the ground, this time raising the broken pieces high into the air. She closed her eyes, feeling each of the splinters and slivers through the spatial connection of her telekinesis. The pieces spun according to her command, positioning the most jagged edge of each piece directly at the Chupacabra. Viv's eyes flung open, and the glass pieces shot in the beast's direction like they were fired from a cannon.

The beast leapt up into the air, dodging the blast of glass by a fraction of a hair. It landed back onto the sand with a booming stomp.

"Viv, please!" Charlotte cried. "Press the button!"

But it was no use. The words didn't get through. The only thing Viv could sense was her enemy, the Chupacabra, through the microscopic pinhole that had burned through the glass shield.

But before Viv could launch a new attack, the creature let out another snapping bark and dug its claws into the sand. It burrowed downward with incredible speed, managing to disappear underground completely within a matter of seconds. Grains of sand poured in to fill the space where the Chupacabra vanished into the dunes below.

Unable to pierce the makeshift glass shelter, the beast had retreated.

It was all over.

But Viv still held up the dome. Her eyes continued to glow green, and her breathing was still rapid, adrenaline coursing through her veins. The power had overwhelmed everything.

The drop of saliva that had broken through Viv's defenses finally singed its way through the metal of her suit. It made contact with her skin, and she felt the searing burn just above her left knee. Her nerve endings slingshotted the pain through her entire body, snapping her mind free from the scorching powers that had been coursing through her veins.

"Viv?" Charlotte said.

Her voice finally cut through the silence. Charlotte poked at her friend's shoulder gently.

"Viv?" she said. "I think it ran off. Are you . . . are you finally back to normal?"

Viv let out an exhale and put down her arms. The tinkling of glass rang like the chimes of a soft rain as the shards fell into messy piles all around them.

Charlotte sprinted over to the spot where the Chupacabra had burrowed down.

"We have to go after it," she said as she stuck her gauntlets into the sand and started digging after it.

"Stand back," Viv said, still feeling the current of power under her skin, even though her mind felt mostly back in focus. Something had shifted when she had let the electric anger overtake her. The power had felt more immediate and easier to control than ever before. Even her voice sounded different somehow. Almost fuller. More resonant.

Charlotte nodded and backed away.

Like a cork from a bottle, Viv lifted the block of sand out of the ground. She set it down a few yards away with a slam, sending a spraying shower of grit up into the air. Charlotte leaned over the gaping hole in the desert floor to see where the beast could've gone.

"It's a long tunnel. Must go down to the VERT Train."

Viv took a few careful steps over the bubbling glass lava and peered down over the ridge, afraid she might see Ernest Becker lying in an injured, tangled mess. She squinted down below, but there was nothing. No trace of him on the empty stretch of sand. Not even an imprint or a trail of footsteps walking away.

It was like he'd vanished into thin air.

"Viv?" Charlotte said.

How is that possible? Where could he have gone?

She scanned her eyes across the sweeping tract of desert before her. But there was no sign of him.

"Viv!" Charlotte cried.

Viv felt the last remnants of heat behind her eyes finally cool. The real world, the dusty wasteland of their surroundings, returned to its normal shades of oranges and reds as the green that had clouded her vision slowly faded away.

"Come on! Let's go!" Charlotte shouted, pointing toward the dark tunnel below. "It's getting away!"

Viv looked down at her own hands. Her fingers still buzzed with the telekinetic powers.

Is this what it's like? Is this what it feels like to have unlimited power?

She thought of her favorite superheroes, all the men and women from the movies, shows, and comic books that she had grown up loving.

Is this what they feel like when they use their abilities?

So . . . out of control?

So . . . inhuman?

The speck of skin above her knee where the saliva had seeped through was marked with a dark blister. Luckily, the metal of the combat suit absorbed most of the toxic heat.

Viv thought back to how she'd been flinging thousands of glass shards like they were bullets, with the ease of flicking a paper football, and how everything else had fallen away. She had completely forgotten about Charlotte, about the button, about anything and everything except taking down her prey. She'd felt barely human.

I really am a monster.

"Viv. Seriously. We need to go after it," Charlotte said. "If that thing gets out of Area 51, people could really get hurt."

She was right. Viv imagined the Chupacabra running loose in downtown Groom Lake, melting people like marshmallows. She let out another sigh and curled her hands into tight fists.

Finding Ernest Becker will have to wait.

Viv nodded at Charlotte, who she noticed for the first time was trying to hide the fact that she was trembling.

My best friend is terrified of me. Good job, Viv. Definitely a monster.

"Should we climb down?" Charlotte asked. "Or could you levitate us with your powers or something?"

Viv shook her head no.

I never want to use those powers again.

She joined Charlotte in overlooking the hole. The desert sun poured into the dark space below, lighting up the first fifty feet. Rungs of cool stainless steel marched all the way down the seemingly mile-long tunnel.

"I guess even the VERT Train needs repairs sometimes,"

Charlotte said, turning around and setting her feet down on the first crossbar.

"Wait," Viv said. "What if the Chupacabra's waiting for us down there? What if it decides to fill the whole tunnel with spit and burn us up to a crisp?"

She watched the realization wash over Charlotte's face.

"Yeah, guess these duplicator gauntlets won't really help against that thing," Charlotte admitted. "You're right. Maybe you should go first."

She climbed back out, giving Viv the go-ahead.

Good. Maybe if that creature decides to roast us alive, I can still protect Charlotte.

Viv looked around one last time at the chaos she'd left in her wake in the desert. To think, it all had started because of stupid Joanna making a move on Elijah. But she couldn't let herself think about that now. She grabbed hold of the ladder and took her first steps down into the darkness.

CHAPTER EIGHTEEN

The Yeti was slower than Elijah originally had expected. Roger ran on all fours; that is, if its lumbering could even be classified as "running." The three of them moved through the snow like a donkey in a swimming pool filled with molasses. Being used to the speed of his flight suit, Elijah felt like he was riding a turtle.

Strange. With how elusive the Yeti seems to be from people's cameras, I always assumed it was lightning quick.

Despite having his assigned cryptid contained and even happy to be returned to the Forbidden Zone, he worried for his friends.

Hope Viv and Charlotte are okay in the desert.

And Ray and Meekee. Oh man, I really hope the Loch Ness Monster is as nice as Roger is.

Sitting high on top of the Yeti's back, Elijah and Joanna clung to the white fur, which at this point was entirely coated with falling snowflakes, making it hard for them to keep their grips. Joanna reached over and grabbed hold around Elijah's waist, trying to steady herself on their bumpy journey.

Elijah glanced back over his shoulder. A massive gray cloud spiraled against the white sky. He could hear the turbulent roar of the new storm approaching on the horizon.

The next blizzard. It's coming faster than we thought.

"Roger?" he asked. "Are we getting close? I think that storm might be catching up to us."

"I think we're close," Roger said. "Should be right up here if my Yeti senses are tingling in the right direction, eh?"

"Wait, stop here," Joanna said.

"Sorry?" Roger said. "What's that you said?"

"Just stop here, please," Joanna asked again.

Roger skidded to a smooth halt.

"Are we there already?" Elijah said.

Joanna jumped off the Yeti's back and landed with a thud. Elijah joined her on the ground, looking around. Their entire surroundings seemed exactly the same as the ice-covered arctic expanse they'd just traversed—completely desolate.

"Eh, sorry, but I'm not sure this is it," Roger said.

"What's wrong, Joanna?" Elijah asked. "Why'd we stop?"

"Look down," Joanna said. "It's an entrance to the VERT Train. All the sectors of the terrarium have one."

Elijah stared at the snow by his feet. It looked like nothing but empty white until he looked a little harder. He tightened his focus and noticed the faint blinking of a red light buried deep beneath the frost.

"Oh, you're right. I see it," Elijah said. "How'd you know where it would be?"

"It was written on the old map that Charlotte found," Joanna said. "I have a photographic memory."

Why am I not surprised?

She wiped away a few inches of snow to reveal a small panel bolted into the permafrost. She typed in a long code, and the blinking red light peeped out a small ding, changing to green.

"There," she said. "I called the train. It should be here any minute."

"The train?" Roger said. "But I thought we were headed to my enclosure hatch?"

"This can get us there," Joanna said, circling around the flickering beacon. "Don't you worry. I'll have you back home in no time."

"Oh gee. I hate to say it, but I'm a bit afraid of trains, eh?"

"Really?" Elijah said. "Why would a huge Yeti be afraid of trains?"

"The same reason anybody would be afraid of trains," Roger said.

"Do you get motion sickness?"

"No. I once had a friend named Leroy. A grizzly bear. He was hunting for some salmon near the tracks one day and got hit. Lost one of his bear legs."

Elijah frowned. "Roger, that's awful. I'm so sorry to hear that."

"I told you Canada's a terrifying place."

A clicking sound tickled Elijah's ears from behind him, and he felt a weight lifted off his shoulders.

Thinking a lump of a snow that was building up on the back of his engine had fallen off, he spun around and saw Joanna holding a metal rotor in her hand. She inspected it in her palm and then tucked it into the inner pocket of her whale coat.

"What are you doing?" Elijah asked, craning his neck to see if the part had slipped out of place from his jetpack. "Did something break?"

"I'm sorry, Elijah," she said. "But I promise I'm doing this for a good reason."

"Sorry? Sorry about what?"

Elijah spun around again like a dog trying to chase its own tail. Something about his flight suit felt wrong. He tried to kick the engine on, but it didn't even sputter. Once more, he tried to activate his wing extensions, but they were completely disabled. The entire flight suit had lost power.

"I'm sorry," she said. "But you're not coming with us."

What?

Elijah's brain couldn't process the words he was hearing. At first, he thought she must be kidding. He smiled, but Joanna's face didn't change one bit. Her eyebrows were slightly pulled together, and her head was tilted to one side. She even looked a little sorry for him.

"I don't understand," Elijah said. "What do you mean?"

"You're staying here in the terrarium while I get Roger out of Area 51."

"Out of Area 51?" Elijah said. "What are you talking about?"

"This poor creature's been trapped here long enough. I'm talking Roger back to Canada. It's only right. It's where a Canadian Yeti belongs."

"Sorry, did you say back to Canada?" Roger chimed in.

"Yes." Joanna's tone was firm. "We're getting you out of this horrible place, and we're never coming back."

"But you've only been working here for a day?" Elijah said. "Don't you like working here?"

"I did," Joanna said. "Until this afternoon, when I realized that Director Harlow and Dr. Frank had been keeping all these poor, innocent creatures locked up for so long."

"Locked up?" Elijah said. "What do you mean 'locked up'?"

Joanna lowered her gaze.

"The Forbidden Zone?" she said. "It's practically a prison."

"A prison? I don't understand. It looked just as good as any other zoo to me?"

"Zoos?" Joanna shuddered at the sound of the word. "Zoos are horrible, too. All those animals were ripped from the wild and forced into those cages. Walking around the Forbidden Zone today, I felt completely sick to my stomach."

She's against zoos? Whoa.

"But they're not animals," Elijah said. "They're cryptids, and they're dangerous. It's totally different."

"What's the difference? Doesn't every creature have the right to live its life peacefully in its own natural habitat?"

"Well, what about FuRo? You keep her in your house all day, don't you?"

"FuRo's a robot. She doesn't have feelings or sensations. That's not a comparable situation," Joanna said. "I would never keep a real living, breathing animal as a pet."

She's anti-pets, too? That's hard-core.

"Joanna, I still don't get it," Elijah said. "Why the heck would you wanna do this?"

"I like to consider myself an eco-warrior. I've started hundreds of petitions to release animals from zoos and other captivity programs. I even busted a few mini horses out of a petting zoo last year," she said. "I'm willing to put myself on the line to defend the defenseless."

"But they're not defenseless; some of these creatures are dangerous," Elijah said. "What if these cryptids are being kept here to protect people from them? Or to protect them from people?"

"Protect them?" Joanna said. "By locking them up and hiding them from the world? By keeping them in a place called the *Forbidden* Zone? It sounds to me like the scientists here wish these animals never even existed in the first place."

Roger let out a whimper.

"So you've been behind all of this?" Elijah said. "You're the one whose been releasing all the creatures?"

Joanna let out a low sigh.

"I hope you'll understand someday. Now, come on, Roger, I'm taking you back to Canada."

"Back to Canada?" Roger said. "Oh well, gee, I'm sorry, but I really don't want to go back there, eh?"

"It's your home. It's where you belong," Joanna said.

"But I like it here," Roger said. "I get plenty of alone time, and you might not believe it, but they treat me just fine."

"But what about the ecosystem?" Joanna said. "The wilderness needs you, Roger. There shouldn't be only one Canadian Yeti left in the wild. You should be out there with a lady Yeti, making beautiful Yeti babies."

"I am a lady Yeti."

Hold on a second.

Elijah snapped out of his confusion for a moment, only to be plunged into another state of bewilderment altogether.

"Wait, what?" Elijah said. "Roger? You're a girl?"

"Last time I checked," Roger replied.

"But . . . we've been calling you Roger?" Joanna said.

"Yeah? It's a nice name." The Yeti nodded. "Listen to it—Raaaahjerrrrr. Cool, right?"

"But . . . you're really big and hairy?" Elijah said.

"A lady can't be really big and hairy, eh?" Roger said. "Sounds sexist to me."

That's a good point.

"You should've seen my mother," Roger continued. "She had a beard down to her knees."

"No matter what kind of beard your mom had, you can't stay here, Roger," Joanna said. "This is no place for a Yeti. It's no place for any creature to be held against their will. We need to get going."

"What's your plan?" Elijah said. "How do you expect to sneak out of here with a ten-ton Yeti?"

"Oh, it's not just the Yeti," she said. "I'm going to help all the imprisoned creatures escape."

All of them? Is she for real?

"You can't do this, Joanna. I won't let you," Elijah said.

"I know it seems bad now," she said. "But trust me. Once we restore all these beautiful animals back into their native territories, you'll see how much balance was missing in the world."

"Sorry, but I'm not sure I really want to go with you," Roger said. "And what about this other small human child? We can't leave him in this kinda cold, eh? He's too skinny to last out here."

"Like I said, I'm sorry, Elijah. But I have to do this."

The VERT Train roared up into the tundra, rising out of the snow like an orca breaching from the sea. The front set of titanium doors opened as the fluorescent light from the train's interior poured in and reflected off the snow, nearly blinding Elijah.

"Sorry, but I am not going with you," Roger said.

Joanna sighed and dug into her coat pocket. She pulled out a little white circle with a gray design, and Elijah immediately recognized what she had.

The control button!

Elijah patted the utility belt by his waist. It was gone.

She pickpocketed me!

Joanna lifted the button into the air and pressed it once with her thumb.

The nanobots worked instantly. Elijah watched as Roger's eyes rolled back in her head. Her massive Yeti body collapsed into the train car with a thud, nearly sending the entire thing off its tracks.

"No!" Elijah said. He reached out toward Roger's colossal, fuzzy foot and tried to tug her back out of the train. It was no use.

"Stop! You can't do this!" he shouted.

But it was much too late. Joanna climbed over Roger's unconscious body and closed the train doors behind her. Elijah barely had time to jump out of the way before the doors slammed shut.

"No!" he shouted again.

Through the glass window, he watched Joanna belt herself into the intricate seat belt straps.

She looked up and mouthed two words:

I'm sorry.

Just as quickly as it appeared, the VERT Train sunk back down into the snow and rocketed away, leaving Elijah stranded.

His flight suit was completely disabled. Now that the thermal lining that had been heating him was switched off, the cold poured in through the orange-and-black mesh like a sieve.

Oh no.

I'm gonna freeze to death out here.

He dug down through the snow, searching for the panel and praying that he could manage to call the train back—to call anything to come save him.

Elijah desperately typed in random numbers, hoping that he might discover his own photographic memory.

But nothing worked. Without the code, he was stuck.

No. No. This can't be happening.

He fell back into the snow on his butt. The cold of the icy ground made his very bones start to shiver.

He wrapped his arms around his legs and folded his head down onto his knees, trying to keep as much of his body heat circulating as possible. But at this rate, considering the temperature and the blizzard that was already on its way, he wasn't sure how much longer he had.

Wait a minute.

His eyes opened in a flash. In that moment, he realized what he'd accidentally rested his chin on.

The wrist communicator!

He popped the small touch screen out of the now-useless shell of his flight suit and turned it on with a switch.

Dad's a genius. If he hadn't been smart enough to make this thing battery operated, I'd really be dead meat.

There was only one person he could reach with this device.

But that one person just might be enough.

Come on, Viv. Please answer.

CHAPTER NINETEEN

The dinging of Viv's wrist communicator echoed through the empty train shaft like the knell of an afternoon church tower. The sound made her want to puke.

No. Please.

Not again.

The light from the screen illuminated her face in the otherwise shadowy tunnel. At this point, they'd passed by dozens of connecting shafts that weaved the VERT Train pathways throughout the terrarium.

"Is that Elijah?" Charlotte asked.

Viv craned her head back and looked up. Charlotte was almost twenty feet above her. She leaned out over the ladder. Between them, a row of clones steadily climbed down, creating a protective barrier for Charlotte in case the Chupacabra made a sneak attack from below.

Not that those clones would last very long if that thing decided it wanted to melt her.

"Yeah," Viv said.

"Answer it," Charlotte said. "I bet they need our help with the Yeti."

Viv thought for a moment, her finger hovering over the button. Two possibilities were waiting for her on the other side of this call.

On the one hand, Viv imagined Elijah cowering beneath the silhouette of a colossal, furry white monster, shaking like a leaf.

But on the other hand, she felt the instant pang of heart-ache imagining yet another scene of Elijah and Joanna cuddling up in the arctic wilderness.

"You really think they're in trouble?" Viv asked.

"Probably," Charlotte replied. "Think about how much trouble we're having with that little Chupacabra. I can only imagine what it would be like to take on a jumbo Yeti."

Viv slammed the screen of the wrist communicator shut, not wanting to take the chance.

If I see even another glimpse of the two of them . . .

I can't deal with that right now.

That first heart-wrenching call was enough to send her into a frenzy. She still felt a bit light-headed from the outburst of Roswellian powers that had overtaken her in the desert.

I can't lose control in here.

She and Charlotte still had a long way to go down the ladder, and Viv didn't want to risk potentially hurting her best friend all because she couldn't keep calm over a boy.

Gotta stay focused. We can't let that Chupacabra escape.

Viv dreaded seeing that freak of nature again. Having to face the beast's onslaught of poisonous saliva in a confined space like this would be a death sentence.

But it has to be down here somewhere.

Claw marks scarred the walls where the creature had scuttled down in a frenzy. A few of the ladder's rungs had been dissolved in several spots, leaving melted holes in the structure. Viv carefully positioned her hands around the weakened points. She mentally crossed her fingers as she climbed, hoping that the overall stability would stay intact. If it didn't, she would be the first one tumbling down that never-ending train shaft.

Her mind drifted for a moment, and she was transported back to recess at her elementary school. The long ladder reminded her of the old playground that she and Charlotte used to play on in the lingering heat of early fall days. So much exposure to the Nevada sun had left the wood warped, and the whole playground was cracked and misshapen. Climbing on it meant splinters were almost a certainty.

Viv looked up. Even if it was a clone's feet above her, for a second, through all of the stress and panic of the day, she felt like she and Charlotte were back at recess, chasing each other around on the jungle gym.

The communicator beeped again, snapping Viv out of her daydream.

"Seriously? Aren't you gonna answer that?" they said like a chorus of voices in her head.

I can't. I can't take the risk.

"No," she said. The ringing of the wrist communicator cut off as Viv slid the cover back over top of the screen as the silence poured back into the train shaft.

Not now.

The quiet got even quieter. The soft, rhythmic clanging of the clones climbing down had stopped. Above Viv's head, each of the Farlottes had frozen in place. She watched as, one by one, they evaporated into the air. All that was left between her and the real Charlotte was a short stretch of darkness.

"What's wrong?" Viv asked.

"Listen."

Charlotte's voice was soft—scared.

Viv stopped her descent and leaned her ear to the cool metal wall. She closed her eyes and focused in, trying to pick up on whatever danger had alerted her best friend's keen ears.

The rung in Viv's hand began to vibrate. Within moments, the entire shaft jolted and rattled.

Charlotte let out a scream as the realization hit her at the exact same time as Viv—there was only one thing that could cause this much commotion.

It's the train!

The LED light attached to the nose cone of the VERT Train lit up the entire tunnel from above. Viv and Charlotte were instantly bathed in a wash of blinding light. The sound was quick to follow. With one hand still gripping the rung of the ladder, Viv instinctively tried to cover her ears with the other. The screeching of the rocket's engine sounded like a marching band blasting Viv's eardrums with a snare.

They'd been wrong to worry about the Chupacabra below. The real danger was coming from above.

The real danger was the train zooming straight toward Charlotte.

No!

As narrow as the tunnel was, even if they flattened themselves down against the ladder, they would still be rocket-train roadkill.

Viv watched in agony as the realization dawned on Charlotte's face and a tear fell down her cheek.

Viv desperately didn't want to use her powers again. Didn't want to feel the inhuman rush of electricity. But she had no choice. With only half a second to react, she felt the surge of energy shoot through her body. Charlotte's life was on the line.

I won't let anything happen to you.

Viv's eyes exploded with green light. This time, the heat of her powers didn't just burn, it ached. She felt the pressure build up behind her eyes like a blazing migraine.

As the train approached, Viv pressed her feet hard into the ladder and sprang backward, letting her instincts guide her. The green glow extended from her body and wrapped a chunk of space in a force field of protective light.

Time seemed to slow down as Viv watched Charlotte's hand slip off the shaking ladder. She fell backward through the air, free-falling like a skydiver who forgot their parachute.

The impossibly fast train appeared out of nowhere. It was inches from colliding with Charlotte's head before her body broke through the seal of the protective telekinetic shield.

Once Charlotte was safely inside, Viv closed her eyes, and yet somehow she could still see everything around her— possibly even clearer now.

The entire train shaft lit up in her mind in a stunning green projection. She could sense every rung of the ladder, every bolt and screw that held the VERT Train together. All of it illuminated in her mind's eye as if she was staring at the blueprints themselves.

She could also see where the train shaft ended below them. And it was coming up fast.

The nose cone pressed against Viv's force field, propelling her and Charlotte down at a blistering speed, still safely enclosed within the shielded bubble.

Viv followed her envisioned map of green light farther down the tunnel.

There.

Just before the bottom of the shaft, where the VERT Train station stood, there was a hollowed-out alcove in the wall covered in burn marks and singes.

That must be where the Chupacabra clawed its way out.

Maybe we can get out there, too.

But she had to time it right. If she moved early, they would smash against the unforgiving walls of the tunnel. But if she moved too late, they would be squished on the bottom of the train shaft like bugs on a windshield.

She waited until the precise moment, eyes still closed, counting each passing nanosecond in her mind.

And then Viv pointed her toes and arched her back as if she was diving into a swimming pool. The telekinetic field moved with her as she pulled Charlotte along. Their orb of green rattled into the compartment, sending them both tumbling out into the hallway just as the VERT Train pulled into the station a few floors below. Its engines switched off with a hiss. Spread out on the floor like a starfish, Viv let out an equally big sigh of relief.

We made it.

We're alive.

They each took a moment to catch their breath. Even though the rumbling of the engine had subsided, Charlotte still vibrated with adrenaline.

"Viv . . . ," she said. "We just rode the *outside* of the VERT Train in an alien bubble?!"

Viv laughed, feeling the fiery heat of her powers fading behind her eyes, though the pounding headache still hammered behind her skull.

"That was by far the best ride on that train I've ever taken!"

Charlotte shouted. "You saved our lives!"

Viv smiled.

Maybe I'm getting better at controlling these powers.

"Come on," Charlotte said, pointing down at the long tracks of melted flooring. "We're close."

Charlotte pulled at her hand, lifting an exhausted Viv up from the ground and toward the stairwell. They hustled down a few flights before they encountered the bright red door left ajar that marked the place where this whole nightmare had begun: the Forbidden Zone.

The circular hall was completely in shambles. Above their heads, panels and wiring hung out of the ceiling as if a tornado had blown through. Many of the glass walls to the enclosures had been completely destroyed and now were lying in heaps of roughly cut shards on the bright red floor.

The wake of the chaos spread out through every square inch of the place. Paw prints, feathers, and scales of all shapes and sizes littered the floor in trails of bizarre debris.

No. How did this happen?

Viv looked around at what was left of the enclosures. The enclosure doors above many had been left open.

Just earlier that day, the Zone had looked so pristine, so well cared for.

We didn't do this . . . Did we?

The coincidence was too great to ignore.

What are the odds that a group of interns sneaked in here this morning and less than twenty-four hours later, it looks like this?

It was quiet. The low hum of busted alarms whined from the walls. Even the security cameras had been torn out of the ceiling with precision.

She and Charlotte instinctively crouched down, hoping to avoid any surprise run-ins.

All these cryptids . . . They must be loose in the compound.

I hope Dr. Frank's team gets here quickly.

A spritely chime shattered the silence. It was Viv's wrist communicator again.

Shoot. He's called three times in a row.

I have no choice. I have to answer.

Viv begrudgingly hit the activate button on her wrist, terrified of what she might see when the screen blinked on.

"Viv!" Elijah's voice erupted from the other end. "Oh! Yes! You answered! I've been trying to reach you for so long!"

Viv cupped her hand around the speaker, trying to muffle the sound as best she could in case any dangerous cryptids were listening in.

"Are you okay?" Viv whispered.

Behind him, a field of pure white enveloped his body from all sides. His hair rustled in the wind, and patches of snow adhered themselves to his eyebrows and in the space below his nose.

"What's going on? You look like you're freezing," Viv said.

"It's Joanna," he said in a hurry. "Joanna's been the one letting all the creatures go."

Viv's eyelids fluttered. It took a few seconds for the words to sink in.

"What? What are you talking about?"

"You can't trust her, Viv," Elijah said. "She's got it in her head that the creatures are all being held against their will. She's been the one releasing them this whole time!"

"You're kidding," Viv said. Charlotte looked back at Viv with wide eyes.

"I'm dead serious," Elijah said, his teeth chattering. "She kidnapped the Yeti!"

Kidnapped the Yeti? How does a girl her size manage to kidnap a Yeti?

"I tried to stop her, but she jumped on the VERT Train and got away!"

The VERT Train . . .

That must've been who just passed us!

Before Viv could respond, movement caught her attention from the corner of her eye. Around the bend of the circle, a familiar figure stood perfectly still.

Viv silently clicked the wrist communicator off and brought her voice down to a nearly imperceptible whisper.

"Charlotte?" Viv said. "Are you using your duplicator gauntlets?"

Charlotte shook her head no.

"Look."

Viv trained her finger toward the individual standing by

the one of the intact enclosures. It was the Californian desert of the thunderbird.

"What is that?" Charlotte said. "Is that supposed to be . . . me?"

The person standing in front of the thunderbird's glass looked like Charlotte, but her skin was white and glossy.

Viv peeked her head around the corner again.

Is that . . . a clone?

Whatever it was, it lifted a white hand and typed in a set of numbers with lightning speed into the touch screen. The glass slid open, leaving nothing but open air between it and the thunderbird perched in its tree.

The strange replica of Charlotte opened its mouth and let out a loud, whistling cry.

The thunderbird squawked back.

"Are they . . . talking?" Charlotte asked. "Did the gauntlet malfunction turn my clone into a freaking bird whisperer?"

The thunderbird extended its gargantuan wings and soared out of the enclosure. Flecks of blue electricity and static sparked off its feathers as it flew straight past Viv and Charlotte and up the staircase, out into the compound.

Just as the thunderbird flew out of view, the real Charlotte leapt out from around the corner.

"Hey! You! Stop right there!" Charlotte shouted, sprinting straight toward her dubious copy.

The replica spun around and grabbed Charlotte by the

shoulders. She could barely get her gauntlets ready by the time it had tossed her into another open enclosure.

The clone punched in another code on the panel and slammed the glass shut.

"NO!" Viv shouted.

She pounced out from behind the rounded corner, but it was too late. The strange version of Charlotte had taken off around the circle, and the real Charlotte was locked inside. She banged on the glass with her duplicator gauntlets.

"Viv! Get me out of here!"

Viv pressed her hands against the glass opposite Charlotte's.

Think, Viv.

"Is the hatch up top open?" Viv said.

"No! Please, Viv! I'm really stuck in here!"

Viv woke the cracked touch screen with her finger. It asked for the security password she didn't know.

How am I supposed to get this open without the code?

If only Charlotte's mom had let her keep the map.

Viv smacked her hand against the glass. She considered blasting it with her arm cannon for a moment, then reconsidered.

That's probably a bad idea.

"Viv?" Charlotte asked. "What's supposed to be in here with me?"

"Let me check."

The red letters on the touch screen appeared a second later:

CRYPTOZOOLOGICAL SUBJECT NO. 10205

MOTHMAN OF WEST VIRGINIA

CLASSIFICATION: LEPIDOPTERA SAPIENS

STATUS: FORBIDDEN IN NORTH AMERICA

"What does it say?"

Viv cocked her head to one side. She'd never heard of it.

"Please!" Charlotte said. "Tell me it's not a *T. Rex*. I promised myself no more *T. Rexes*."

"Well . . . it's not a *T. Rex*," Viv said.

"Then what is it?!"

"It says . . . um, Mothman?"

Charlotte's face contorted into a prickly scowl.

"Mothman? What does that mean? Like a little bug guy?"

Viv swiped her finger across the touch screen. The info card slid over and revealed a terrifying image—a black, hunched silhouette of a winged creature with round, red eyes and sharp, gargoyle-esque talons.

"Your face looks bad. Is it bad?" Charlotte said.

Viv snapped her head toward her left. The white clone had finished releasing a final few cryptids and was now sprinting up the staircase.

This is my only chance.

"I'll come back for you!" Viv shouted over her shoulder. "I promise!"

"No, Viv! Please don't leave!" Charlotte banged her fist against the glass.

The Farlotte disappeared up the first set of stairs. Viv

sprinted as fast as she could, trying to keep up.

No. It can't be.

Beneath the single light that was still intact, she watched the shadowy silhouette of the Charlotte replica morph back into a pint-size ferret. Just like when the robot had transformed in the arena during their battle, the white plates unraveled and folded in on themselves like intricate origami.

She'd caught FuRo in the act.

Elijah was right. It isn't a rogue clone.

Joanna is *the one behind all of this.*

In the arena, the robot had no problems transforming into all sorts of different creatures and forms. There was only one reason why FuRo would've been programmed to take the shape of her best friend.

Joanna's been trying to frame Charlotte.

Viv hustled up the stairs after FuRo, her eyes prickling with the start of fury.

This is my only shot.

I have to stop her.

CHAPTER TWENTY

In soaking wet clothes, the air vents were even colder than Ray remembered.

Geez. Why can't I get through one week working at this place without getting drenched in sludge and stuck in the airshaft?

He crawled on his hands and knees, trying to get his bearings from the narrow slits in the grates beneath his fingers, but so far he didn't recognize any of the rooms below.

Meekee skipped along cheerfully in front of him, seemingly happy to be in a "hallway" that was relatively Meekee size.

"Meekee?" Ray said. "Thank you for saving my life and all, but—"

"Meekee!"

"Why didn't you tell me that you had supersecret powers?"

"Meekee!" the little alien replied.

"Yeah," Ray said. "I thought that's what you'd say."

He couldn't help but smile as they made their way back to what Ray hoped was the main pavilion.

They crawled along in silence for a while. Ray's pants were starting to ride up in all sorts of uncomfortable places.

"Boy, I'm gonna be so chafed after this," Ray said. "Do you know that word, Meekee? Try to say it. 'Chafed.'"

The alien gave a butt wiggle and opened his mouth.

"Meekee?"

"Hmm. Let's try something else," Ray said. "What about 'creaky'? That's pretty close. These air vent panels are creaky. Can you say 'creaky'?"

Meekee stopped in his tracks. Ray stopped, too.

"Cree . . ."

"Yeah?" Ray encouraged. "Keep going!"

"Cree . . ."

He's so close!

Just then, Meekee's antenna shot up into the air and twitched back and forth. The little alien curled up into a ball, letting out another high-pitched growl.

"What's wrong, buddy?" Ray asked. "We don't have to practice now if you don't want to."

But Meekee was focused on something else—the shadows of movement from below the airshaft had caught his attention.

What's got him so upset?

Ray shimmied over to the grate Meekee was standing on and pressed his eyes against the cold strips of metal.

His jaw would've fallen straight through and onto the floor if it could've.

A parade of outlandish and breathtaking creatures marched through the corridor beneath them.

Prickly green bobcats chased one another across the floor, leaving rolling piles of needles in their wake. Behind them, a group of mice with absurdly long tails skittered together in one giant huddle. In total synchronicity, the rodents leapt up into the air, creating a dazzling display of gymnastic backflips and twirls that left Ray in awe.

Strange monkeys bounded into his view. Then a troop of impish gremlins hopped by on the back of a worm so colossal, it took up the entire hallway. A pack of wolves all standing up on their hind legs were quick to follow.

Whoa!

But Ray's momentary wonder was shattered.

Tottering just behind the horned horses, a congregation of alligators scraped their big bellies across the ground. They writhed and snapped at one another. Each had an "I ♥ New York" sticker among other litter pressed into their backs. Humongous snapping turtles followed them, waddling by with their imposing jaws.

Then Ray felt his stomach shrivel up in his gut. He was hit by the smell first, an odor so foul and rotten, it reminded him of the time his dad had accidentally forgotten about an egg roll in the fridge in their garage. Apparently, the egg roll had been there since 2018.

Gross!

Ray's eyelids fluttered with despair as the source of the noxious stench came sauntering into his view.

The beast was a monstrous sight. A deer skull served as its head, and a massive spread of bony antlers extended out. Its emaciated fingers led to a set of lengthy claws, and its knees bent backward at an angle that made it look like they'd been purposefully broken.

Ray had never seen something so terrifying, something that looked like death incarnate.

The monster's rib cage was exposed through the ashen gray ribbons of skin. It sounded like its very bones were scraping against each other.

"Creaky!" Meekee cheeped.

The skeletal, deerlike humanoid snapped upright at the sound.

Ray clapped his hand over the little alien's face, trying to muffle the language he so desperately had been trying to teach him.

Ray's heart all but stopped in his chest. The creature's empty, pale white eyes were sunken deep into their sockets. They stared up at the ceiling, directly at Ray and Meekee through the vent.

Ray didn't even dare to breathe. Had a doctor been examining him at this very moment, he might've been packed up in a body bag and headed to the morgue.

The monster let out a whistling howl so strong, Ray felt his hair blow back in the breeze through the grate. The smell stank like flesh and decaying fruit. It nearly singed off his eyebrows.

The creature filed back in line, rejoining the cavalcade as the rest of the cryptids marched farther down the hall.

If he hadn't already emptied his bladder in the Loch Ness Monster's wave pool, Ray would've peed himself again.

Once the procession of terrifying, magnificent creatures had exited into the next corridor and far from his view, Ray unclasped his hand from over Meekee's face. The extraterrestrial took in a gasping wheeze of air.

Sorry!

Ray took some solace in the fact that the beasts were all headed in the opposite direction as he was, back toward where he'd encountered the Loch Ness Monster.

But still, the sight of that last monster was enough to give him nightmares for months.

He and Meekee continued their crawl, but this time, not a single word was exchanged. They took random turns right and left. Ray checked every slat below his fingers for any sign of that horrifying creature.

He trembled with every plodding stride and eventually closed his eyes, trying to think happy thoughts.

He felt something fuzzy brush up against his finger. Meekee was holding his hand.

Aw! He's comforting me. Whatta good boy.

Ray pressed his lips together and cupped his other hand around Meekee.

"Ya know what, buddy?" Ray said. "You're my best friend."

Meekee looked up at him with his big, almond-shaped eyes.

"Ray . . . ," Meekee said. "Best . . . friend?"

Ray jumped up with excitement and banged his head on the top of the airshaft.

Did I hear that right?

"Meekee?" Ray exclaimed. "Meekee, what did you just say?!"

"Best friend!" the little alien pipped again.

"Meekee! You said a whole sentence! Oh, I knew you could do it!" Ray said with proud, fatherly tears in his eyes. "Do you really mean it?"

"Best friend! Best friend!" Meekee repeated.

"I'll take that as a yes!"

Ray scooped Meekee up into his arms and pressed the alien's warm, fuzzy cheek against his.

"Ray!" Meekee said.

"Meekee!" Ray said.

"RAY!" Meekee said.

"MEEKEE!" Ray said.

Meekee wrapped himself around Ray's face, licking at his nose. Ray giggled and tried to pry the little guy off, but it quickly turned into a rowdy tickle fight. Ray scratched at Meekee's belly, sending his four legs kicking wildly through the air like a puppy.

Meekee wrestled his way out of Ray's grasp and tackled him again, this time sending Ray tumbling back in the airshaft. His left buttock collided with one of the vent covers screwed into the panels, and the grate gave way below them.

Ray crashed down from the ceiling and landed in a heap on the floor. The impact against the hard steel floor sent a shooting pain up through his pelvis.

He let out a long groan.

Can't believe I just busted my butt!

Meekee landed on top of Ray's face. Ray peeled the little alien from his forehead and gently set him on the ground. Ray wiped his wet hair out of his face and looked up.

A tall set of legs stood above him.

"AHH!" Ray screamed and slid back across the floor on his tender hip.

He rubbed at his eyes, trying to reset his vision under the harsh light of the pavilion.

Please don't be a monster. Please don't be a monster.

But it wasn't a monster.

It was a low pair of heels that led up to a gray pencil skirt.

"Raymond?"

It was Director Harlow. She folded her arms across her chest, tapped her foot, and gave him a dissatisfied look.

Oh crud.

CHAPTER TWENTY-ONE

Director Cassandra Harlow had been tucked in her bed when it had happened. She'd just finished reading the latest scientific journal on robotics and was drifting off to sleep. Then the call came in from Dr. Frank. It was an emergency signal—one that Cassandra had never received in all her time working at the compound.

And now, to add more confusion to the whole ordeal, Ray Mond had just fallen out of the ceiling.

The boy stood up in a hurry, grabbing at his backside. He dripped with some sort of dirty water, leaving a puddle on the ground in the shape of his body.

"Director Harlow!" Ray said, throwing his arms around her. "Thank goodness! I was hoping you'd come!"

What on Earth?

"Ray, what are you doing here?" she asked.

"It's a very long story."

A green ball of damp fluff sat on the floor beside him.

"Meekee!"

Heavens.

She lifted the little alien off the floor and tried to warm him up against her chest. He cuddled into her collarbone and purred.

"Ray? Why is Meekee not in his bed?" she asked.

"I, uh, I, well—"

"You know the rules."

While Ray was continuing to stammer out some excuse, Dr. Frank came sprinting out of her office.

"Sabrina," Director Harlow said. "What in the world is happening?"

"I'm still conducting my investigation," Dr. Frank replied. "But it seems we had an intruder at some point tonight between oh two hundred and oh three hundred hours this morning."

An intruder?

In all her years, an intruder was unheard of. Sure, the errant fanatic would occasionally wander into the area, following their own convoluted GPS coordinates. But with the high-tech cloaking mechanism that shrouded the entire base to look like more Nevada desert, no one had ever gotten close to breaking in.

"And how many of the creatures are out of their enclosures?" she asked.

"As of my last check, of the one hundred and four cryptids kept in the Forbidden Zone, eighty-seven creatures are currently unaccounted for. The rest of the Extra-Normal Affairs team is on their way, but we must act sooner rather than later."

Dr. Frank opened a briefcase and showed her the white control buttons, arranged in immaculate fashion.

But something was wrong. Three were missing.

Director Harlow surveyed the silhouettes on each of the buttons and immediately knew which weren't present in their slots.

"Where are the control buttons for the Chupacabra, the Yeti, and the Loch Ness Monster?" Director Harlow asked.

"I gave them to the interns," Dr. Frank said.

"The interns?" Director Harlow said. "Why were the interns called here? They're clearance level one. They shouldn't know about any of this in the first place."

"I certainly didn't call them."

"Then who did?"

Dr. Frank sighed and cleared her throat before continuing.

"It was Charlotte. It seems that she might've been our intruder."

Charlotte? No. It can't be.

What a disaster. Now I see why Viv ended up here before I did.

"You should've dismissed them straightaway," Director Harlow said.

"My apologies, director. I thought I could repair the defense mechanism and they could contain the creatures before it became a problem," Dr. Frank said.

"Seems like we may be past that point," Director Harlow said. "If we make it out of this, I want a full incident report on my desk by tomorrow morning."

Director Harlow had been friends with Sabrina Frank for over a decade. She never took pleasure in reprimanding any of her employees, but it particularly stung when it was a long-time, trusted confidante.

"Any ideas where my daughter is?" Director Harlow asked.

"Yes. I last spotted her and Charlotte on the security cameras exiting the VERT Train near Platform 64L. They were hot on the Chupacabra's tail."

Cassandra's heart twisted with dread.

As many creatures as she'd encountered during her time at Area 51, few were as fearsome and as formidable as the goat-sucking fiend. She remembered the day that the Extra-Normal Affairs team had captured it in rural Puerto Rico. They'd been requested by the Latin American field office to detain the Chupacabra to preserve the local livestock population and protect civilians.

Not only did the beast have acidic saliva, but the field office had alleged stories of the creature using mind control when it was particularly hungry or distressed. Though Director Harlow had never seen it before, as they'd been sure to keep the Chupacabra very comfortable during its time there, the creature was supposedly capable of rendering its targets into puppets, being able to control their every physical movement against the victim's wishes.

Viv's in danger.

Her sense of professionalism was immediately taken over by her maternal instincts. She snapped into action mode.

Our primary goal should be containment.

Director Harlow turned to the unlikely duo beside her.

"Where are the released creatures now?"

"I just saw them!" Ray said. "From up in the air vents a few corridors in that direction. I passed a whole horde!"

"What did you see?" Dr. Frank said.

"All sorts of things! Cats? Mice? Alligators? I'm not even sure what I saw!" Ray said. "And there was . . . um, and . . ."

The boy seemed to fold in on himself, scared to even speak into existence whatever he'd seen.

"And what, Ray?" Director Harlow pressed.

"I don't know what it was, but it was super scary. Like a walking deer skeleton with huge antlers and scary white eyes?"

The windigo. Another extremely dangerous creature.

"That's strange . . . ," Dr. Frank said. "The windigo only reveals itself to the weak and vulnerable."

"Oh, well, that's just great," Ray said. "Way to really boost my confidence, windigo."

"Right now, we only have one option," Director Harlow said. "I want the priority to be finding all the escaped cryptids, particularly those threat level four and above, and returning them to a secure holding location."

She made her way over to the computer panel on the wall and plunged her hands down into the orb of the Central Brain. The red scanning light instantly recognized her palm prints, and the cluster of floating hologram screens extended from the wall.

"Initiate lockdown procedure eight-eight-three-five-one." She turned to Dr. Frank. "Next, we'll need the last three buttons."

"Ray?" Dr. Frank turned to the shivering boy. "Give Director Harlow your control button."

Ray shuffled his soggy feet along the floor. Meekee leapt from Director Harlow's shoulder onto Ray, scampering around the boy's torso. The little alien perched himself on top of Ray's shoulder.

"I, uh . . . I lost it," he muttered.

"You lost it?" Dr. Frank gave him one of her devastating, icy glares. "What do you mean you lost it?"

"I'm sorry!" Ray said. "Everything happened so fast! It's such an itty-bitty button, and the waves were so big."

Director Harlow's head snapped upright.

The waves? That can only mean one thing.

"Waves? What waves?" Dr. Frank said.

Ray gave her a petrified look, eyes filling up with salty water.

"You didn't tell me the Loch Ness Monster was gonna be huge!" Ray whined.

"It's not. The Loch Ness Monster is one of the only creatures in this galaxy that has compressible volume. It can expand to fit the size of whatever body of water it's in," Dr. Frank said. "Why do you think the Scots sent it over in a fishbowl?"

Director Harlow had nearly forgotten.

Perfect. Now, the entire government of Scotland is going to want my head.

"Ray? You're saying the room filled with water?"

"Yes! That's what I came to tell you, Dr. Frank! Somebody that looked a lot like Charlotte locked me in there while the whole thing became a swimming pool!"

Director Harlow wanted to kick herself.

She'd considered this possibility. Especially after the events of last week, she wanted to prepare the base to avoid another potentially massive meltdown. In fact, she had been planning on creating a new security system that, when needed, could activate the nanobots within every creature they kept in the Forbidden Zone all at once.

I should've done it sooner. The buttons aren't enough.

But she'd never imagined them all getting loose at the same time.

We need to act.

"Sabrina? Be ready with those control buttons. We can't wait any longer for the rest of the team. It's now or never."

Director Harlow whipped open her coat and revealed two plasma pistols tucked into each interior pocket. After the Roswellians had broken out last week, she'd decided to always keep one on her, even if it was against Area 51 protocol.

As much as she didn't want to admit it, she hadn't truly felt safe on the base since the aliens had gotten loose. Her daughter was almost kidnapped while she'd been taken prisoner, and she never wanted to feel that helpless again.

This is only for protection. To protect Viv.

She tossed one to Dr. Frank, who raised a curious brow.

"Only use this in case of emergency," she instructed.

Dr. Frank nodded.

"What about me, Director Harlow? What should I do?" Ray asked.

"Ray, I want you and Meekee to stay here in the main pavilion," she said. "This is far too dangerous for an intern to be involved—"

But they were too late. A sizzling blast erupted from the west end of the pavilion. A fiery breach in the wall crackled and fizzled as a beast with sickly skin crawled out and along the ceiling, its long tail slashing back and forth in a rhythmic sway.

It was the Chupacabra. Its eyes radiated heat, glimmering with a red inferno.

And it wasn't alone.

Through the newly burned hole, an army of cryptids came pouring into the room. Swamp creatures, wampus cats, skunk apes, and Fresno night crawlers came marching in, each of them, strangely enough, with eyes radiating the same red light as the Chupacabra's.

It's much worse than I thought. The compound's been completely overrun.

"There are too many of them!" Ray cried.

Not while I'm here.

Director Harlow lifted the lid off the briefcase in Dr. Frank's outstretched arms and zeroed in. She pressed the button for the swamp creatures first. Within seconds, their eyes rolled back into their heads. The six of them collapsed against the floor with a thud, instantly falling into a deep sleep.

Next was the thunderbird. It swooped into the room at a blistering speed. The bird's normally majestic, sapphire gaze was now a sickening shade of crimson. The thunderbird was typically a peaceful and docile animal, but today it seemed different. Aggressive. It circled the ceiling and discharged bolts of lightning in their direction, letting out squawks of fury as it maneuvered through the room.

Director Harlow located its corresponding button in the briefcase and pressed it. The feathered beast curled up into a ball in midair, rolled onto the floor, and finally came to rest by a set of tables next to the elevator shaft.

One by one, with every button that she and Dr. Frank pulled out and pressed, the cryptids were knocked unconscious, just as they'd hoped. The myriad of beasts piled up near the open wall in slumbering heaps.

Director Harlow let out a momentary exhale.

The buttons are going to work. We can do this.

But there was still one creature looming.

Its growling hiss came from directly above them on the ceiling. Drops of scorching liquid fell around Ray's feet. He pranced around trying to avoid each deadly ball of spit. He hollered with panic with every step.

The Chupacabra.

Director Harlow reached back into the briefcase.

Shoot!

She'd forgotten that Viv and Charlotte still had the button they needed. And the girls were nowhere to be seen.

Injuring any of the cryptids went against all protocol at the base, but Director Harlow didn't see any other option.

This is life or death.

She aimed her pistol and fired up toward the ceiling, trying at first to simply scare the creature. Concrete rained down on them, but the beast seemed undisturbed. Instead of scampering off, the Chupacabra dropped onto the floor a few feet in front of them, snarling with each step closer to Dr. Frank.

Just then, its eyes erupted with two beacons of red light. The beams shot across the room and connected with Dr. Frank's eyes.

All at once, her irises had turned the same bright red. The color of blood.

"Sabrina?" Director Harlow said, reaching out her hand.

But she was too late.

Dr. Frank turned the plasma pistol in her hand around, aiming it directly at Director Harlow.

The rumors are true.

Whatever the Chupacabra had done to Dr. Frank with that stare, she had now become its human puppet.

"No!" Director Harlow said. "Fight it, Sabrina! I know you can!"

"Cassandra!" Dr. Frank shouted, straining against the

Chupacabra's command. "I'm sorry!"

Her finger pulled down on the trigger, and the blast from the plasma pistol soared through the air.

Director Harlow stood frozen for just a moment, but it was one moment too long. She closed her eyes as the blue beam traveled straight toward her.

Ray tackled her to the ground milliseconds before the blast made contact. They slid across the floor in a clump.

Did Ray Mond just save my life?

Dr. Frank struggled, trying to drop the weapon she was no longer in control of.

Director Harlow took advantage of her confusion to hustle Ray toward the same air vent that he, Charlotte, and Viv had used to escape from the Roswellians last week.

"Really? I'm going BACK into the airshaft?" Ray said. "What's a kid gotta do to catch a break?!"

"Yes!" she shouted. "Just for now!"

She tucked him and Meekee inside, slammed the grate shut, and spun back around to face her foe.

The Chupacabra howled with rage. Its red gaze swept across the room like a laser beam, trying to take control of whatever living creature crossed its path.

Director Harlow ducked, rolling out of the way just in time.

This is going to be harder than I thought.

CHAPTER
TWENTY-TWO

Viv was hot on FuRo's trail, but the slinky robot was quicker than she expected, skittering around every corner of the compound and always staying a few turns in front of her. FuRo's metallic body nearly disappeared against the titanium floor, making it extra tough for Viv to keep up.

They'd climbed who knows how many steps leaving the Forbidden Zone, and Viv was starting to feel the ache take over her muscles.

She tried to call upon her powers, hoping that she'd be able to levitate herself toward the main floor. But they never came.

Of course. Right when I need them, these stupid powers refuse to kick in.

She was exhausted and completely out of breath. Viv turned another corner, and whatever little air she had left in her lungs tightened up at the sight of the creatures before her.

No way.

It was a pair of horses, trotting by in the hallway as if they were in a flowery meadow. Their manes had every color Viv had even seen and then some. There was jack-o'-lantern orange leading into canary yellow by their ears, and even a tress of neon turquoise spilled down their backs. But most striking was the sparkly horn atop each of their heads that shimmered as they clip-clopped past her. For a moment, Viv felt like she was in a dream.

Unicorns are real, too?!

FuRo scampered past, escaping her view. Viv snapped out of her daze, and she suddenly realized where the little troublemaker had been leading her.

We're right outside the main pavilion! That must be where they're all trying to escape!

Strange sounds were coming from inside. Viv tried to push open the door manually, but it was sealed tight.

The intercom system above the door rang to life. The voice was calm, friendly even: "Lockdown procedure eight-eight-three-five-seven-one initiated. Please stay sheltered in place until further notice."

Darn.

Viv banged her fists on the door, but it wouldn't open. She leaned her head against the cool steel. The noises coming from inside were raucous, a mix of inhuman cries, roars, and bursts.

I need to get in there.

She loaded up a blast in her arm cannon, ready to fire at the locking mechanism on the doors, but just as she was about to release the trigger, movement caught her eye from the periphery of her vision.

It was FuRo again, this time crawling into the main pavilion through a hole that had been blown into the wall. Her little white butt wiggled as she scurried in through the breach.

There!

Viv followed suit. She climbed up the melted mess of metal, jumped through to the other side, and skidded out into the pavilion.

Oh. Oh no.

The hall had descended into pure chaos. Dozens of creatures ran rampant in the main hall. Winged beasts circled high above in the air. Weird-looking monkeys swung from the lights and panels hanging from the ceiling. Along the floor, reptiles, rodents, and bugs of all shapes and sizes squirmed by—each set of eyes smoldering with an angry red glow.

It was as if somebody had taken an evil zoo, flipped it upside down, and dumped all of its contents out.

Near the back wall, a familiar face struggled against the onslaught.

"Mom?!"

The word jumped out of Viv's chest before she could stop it. She wanted to run over and wrap her mother in a hug, but her outburst had caught the attention of another creature: the Chupacabra.

It stood hunched over one of the large desks in the center of the room. Viv had never seen eyes so red, like the color of a polished ruby. She shielded her face away from the blinding light.

The beast growled in recognition as its gaze settled on her.

"Viv!" her mom yelled out. "Quick! The button!"

Right!

Viv almost completely forgot about why she and Charlotte had even set out in the first place. She pawed around at her belt. Tucked into her combat suit, miraculously, the little white button was still there.

She held it out toward the creature and pressed down hard.

It had no effect.

I don't understand.

Viv pressed the button again.

The Chupacabra curled up its lips, revealing a jagged row of teeth as if it was smiling back at her.

Why isn't this working?!

The Chupacabra leapt down from the table and flicked its tongue back and forth, eyeing Viv like a piece of raw meat.

Suddenly, Ray's head poked out of an air vent near the back wall.

"Viv!" he shouted. "Over here!"

"Ray?"

Though it had only been a few hours, she felt like it had been days since they'd last seen each other.

"It's the mind control!" he shouted. "Don't stare into the Chupacabra's eyes!"

He pointed across the pavilion, toward another figure that Viv hadn't yet noticed. It was Dr. Frank, but her back was turned to Viv.

"Viv!" Director Harlow shouted from across the room. "Watch out!"

Dr. Frank slowly turned around. Her eyes were cherry red, just like the Chupacabra's.

What is she doing?

She aimed her plasma pistol directly at Viv.

"Vivian," her voice trembled. "I'm so sorry."

"No! Don't!" Viv shouted.

Viv watched as Dr. Frank's finger started to pull down on the trigger. Viv dove to her left as her mom grabbed Dr. Frank's wrist and twisted it.

Viv hit the ground and slid back toward the hole in the wall where she'd climbed in. She felt the anger boiling up behind her eyes.

No! I have to keep calm!

With her mom, Ray, and Dr. Frank there, if she lost control now, it'd be all over.

My secret would be out.

"Viv!" her mom said. "Go! Get out of here! It's too dangerous!"

"I'm not leaving you!"

"I'm not giving you a choice, Vivian!" her mom shouted back.

Viv glanced up at the hole she'd entered through just in time to see a large shadow pass in the corridor. She didn't want to leave her mom behind, but after another insistent shout, she climbed back up and peered down the hall.

Joanna.

She was perched high on top of the shoulders of the biggest gorilla Viv had ever seen.

What the heck is that? Is that even a gorilla?

The beast's fur was completely white, and it was so tall, its head nearly brushed against the ceiling as they plodded down the corridor.

It clicked together in Viv's mind.

The Yeti!

They're trying to escape!

"Joanna!" she called out. "Stop!"

Joanna glanced over her shoulder at Viv.

"Run, Roger! Come on!" Joanna called out, smacking the Yeti on its back.

Huh? Roger?

"Faster! Faster!" Joanna shouted, an edge of fear tinging her voice. It almost sounded like they were running from something else.

What could possibly be chasing them?

As big as it was, the massive Yeti was relatively slow. Joanna leapt down from its shoulders, trying her best to drag the giant beast farther down the hall.

The sound hit Viv first. She spun on her heels just in time to see what they were running from.

A wall of water exploded from around the corner.

What?!

The tidal wave must've already traveled through most of the compound. It was littered with debris. Papers from the old copy room sloshed around in waterlogged clumps on the surface. There was even a silver serving tray from the cafeteria acting as a makeshift lifeboat for a few lucky jackalopes.

Viv had never seen so much water in her life. She didn't even know that Nevada had this much water in the entire state.

She took off running as fast as she could.

Come on, powers! Now would be a good time!

But her Roswellian abilities still wouldn't work. She was on her own, relying solely on her already weary human legs.

What changed? I felt so in control back in the tunnel!

It only took a few seconds for the swell of water to crash into her. Viv was instantly swept off her feet and carried away down the corridor. Joanna and the Yeti were soon to follow.

The flood swept into the pavilion, picking up everything in its path. It was unstoppable. The water carried Viv, all the creatures, Director Harlow, and Dr. Frank out into the compound.

With the lockdown protocol already initiated, all the doors were tightly shut. They moved like they were in a funnel, following the natural slope of the compound.

Viv fought against the waves. Every time her head broke the surface, she tried to survey the hallway as they rode the torrent still pouring in.

From the looks of it, this water isn't going to stop anytime soon.

And then, like a bolt of lightning from the thunderbird, the idea hit her all at once.

I know a place that can hold this much water.

She reached out her right arm and shot at the control panel above the door at the end of the hallway.

Just a few more turns, and we can make it!

With the lockdown still in place, Viv had to strategically blast the control panels on each door they approached. With every zap, the wall of water was diverted closer and closer to her destination.

Joanna. The Yeti. The Chupacabra. Her mom. Dr. Frank.

One by one, Viv led the entire crowd floating in the water toward the place where she planned to finish this once and for all.

The arena.

❋ ❋ ❋ ❋ ❋

Ray was sick of being in air vents. He was also sick of being wet.

Are all internships like this?!

He had retreated back into the vents after Viv had left the main pavilion, but by the time of the rush of water started to fill his small compartment, he knew he needed to make a move—and fast.

The vent sloshed more with every second, and the water was just like he'd remembered it: cold and gritty.

Not again!

He reared his legs back and kicked out from the vent with all his might. Meekee clung to the top of his head, pulling at locks of Ray's hair to stay above the waterline.

The two were once again dragged out in the undertow. They tumbled around until they were eventually pulled out into the hallway. He and Meekee brought up the back of the pack. In the water in front of them, Ray saw a whole assortment of creatures tumbling around atop the waves.

Phew. At least I don't see the Loch Ness Monster.

On second thought, better to see the Loch Ness Monster than that horrifying Chupacabra.

He felt something grab hold of him beneath the surface.

"AHHH!" He let out a bloodcurdling scream.

No! Please! I didn't mean it!

For a split second, he thought it was Nessie, coming to collect the little boy that it wanted to eat earlier. But the arm wrapped around his waist was covered in a friendly purple suit.

Viv!

She'd somehow managed to hold on to one of the hallway control panels and grabbed him before he was swept into the next room. The water spiraled around them as they became the only eddy in the rushing river.

"Ray! Ray! Ray!" Meekee shouted from on top of his head.

"Meekee, not now!" Ray shouted back. "We'll talk later!"

"Ray! Ray! Ray!" The little alien refused to give up. Meekee's eyes were pleading as he pointed two of his four legs toward something a few yards away in the water.

On the crest of one of the rocking waves, a tiny speck of blue stuck out from all the rest.

It was the growth ray, floating by on the surface.

Oh! He means the growth *ray! Good thinking, Meekee!*

He reached out and scooped up the gadget just before it floated past.

"I can't hold on much longer," Viv said. "Are you ready?"

Ray nodded and held his breath. As Viv let go of her grip, Ray was pulled in backward. He got one last glance down the hallway before they tumbled through the walkway, over the rows of auditorium seats, and into the basin of the arena below.

They weren't the last to arrive.

A massive, looming shadow was speeding through the waves toward them, and Ray recognized the silhouette instantly.

There it is.

The Loch Ness Monster was the final creature to enter the arena. It snapped its jaws up at the gargoyles and Pegasus flying around the room.

Ray watched the giant beast lick its lips, instead deciding to go for an easy meal—all the unconscious creatures floating on the surface.

No! Nobody's getting eaten on my watch!

Ray pulled the trigger on the growth ray. He felt the electricity zap through his fingertips and shoot down through his legs. His body expanded until, remarkably, his feet could touch the ground.

"Ray! Ray! Ray!" The tiny speck that was Meekee still clinging to his hair cheered him on.

The Loch Ness Monster curled back and bellowed at the only other thing in the room even close to its size.

Ray smiled, knowing this time their battle would be much more of a fair fight.

* * * * *

Though his teeth chattered and his toes felt like they might've fallen off somewhere along the way, Elijah had made it out of the tundra of the terrarium through the Yeti's enclosure door and back into the warmth of the main floor.

He was looking forward to getting out of his icicle-covered flight suit and into some comfortable clothing, but as soon as he stepped out into the corridor, his hopes were immediately dashed.

Oh great.

A flood of rippling, surging water rushed toward him. The volume nearly filled up the entire hallway.

He braced himself, but the waves were too strong, and he

was swept up into the current like a piece of driftwood.

The waves pulled him through the halls. He tried to cling to a stabilizing surface, but with his fingers still numb, he couldn't hold on to anything.

Before Elijah knew it, he was swirling into the arena like flushed toilet water.

The pool was busy with life. Cryptids were strewn across every inch of the arena. Elijah managed to snag himself on one of the rows of chairs. He fought against the water, climbing up each level until he was safely above the waterline.

After a moment to catch his breath, he realized he wasn't alone up there.

Next to him, a soggy white mass clung to the highest row of seats.

"Roger?" Elijah said.

The Yeti peered down at him with a friendly smile and a wave of her gargantuan paw.

"Other small human child?" Roger said. "Good to see you! How's it going, eh?"

"Roger! What are you doing?" Elijah said.

"I'm not sure," Roger said. "I remember being in the snow but then after that, nothing. When I woke up, Joanna said that she was taking me away."

Two beams of red light hurled down from the ceiling. Roger looked up to investigate. Her eyes were instantly overtaken by the blood-colored gleam.

Elijah followed her gaze. A grotesque, skinny creature clung to the ceiling. One by one, its red eyes zapped the faces of other cryptids in the arena.

What the heck is it doing?

When he looked back, Roger's fist was smashing down through the air right at him. Elijah dodged out of the way just in time. Her paws hammered into the seats he had just been holding on to. The wood and fabric splintered into a million pieces.

"Roger?" Elijah yelled. "What are you doing?!"

"So sorry!" Roger shouted, her eyes still glowing red. "Gee, not sure what's wrong with me! I don't seem to be in control!"

She lifted her arms again, pulling back for another attack.

"Roger! Please!"

Elijah couldn't believe his eyes.

Is this really happening?

Am I about to get punched by a Yeti?

CHAPTER
TWENTY-THREE

Viv's chest crashed into a large object as she toppled through the water, again. She had already run into a myriad of creatures while being dragged through the current into the arena, some wildly thrashing in the waves and others still knocked out from their control buttons.

Whatever hit her felt solid; way too sturdy to be a living thing.

The podium.

It was the same one that Joanna had knocked her off from yesterday. The steel column was steady, by far the most stable thing in the swirling pool of chaos.

Viv wrapped her arms around it using every ounce of strength she had left and started to climb her way up. The water gurgled around her, threatening to pull her back in if her hands slipped for even a single moment.

If she fell now, Viv wasn't sure she'd have enough energy to try again.

I can do it. I know I can.

She pulled and pulled, slowly and carefully shinnying herself up the tall column of steel. The added weight from the water in her combat suit didn't help, either. The body armor had filled up so much, she felt like a human ladle.

Yes! I'm so close!

Viv wrapped her fingers around the edge of the podium and hoisted herself up.

Thankfully, the ink from FuRo's squid blasts had already been scraped off, otherwise she would've tumbled back into the ravenous ocean below.

From her new vantage point this high up, Viv could see just how disorderly and nightmarish the arena really was.

Creatures from all walks of life—land, sea, and sky—formed a turbulent whirlwind of destruction.

Viv peered down, seeing for the first time what looked like a group of women with long hair and even longer fish tails circling in the water around her podium.

Mermaids are real, too?

As soon as the thought even crossed her mind, all three of the women snapped their heads up and glared at her. Their eyes gleamed with a menacing red, a look that sent shivers down Viv's spine. Each of the women opened their mouths and bared four rows of pointy, jagged shark's teeth.

Yikes! They're nothing like the mermaids I imagined.

In fact, nearly every eye in the arena was glowing bright red under the Chupacabra's twisted influence.

The noise in the arena was even more frightening than the sights. Below, the water sloshed like juice in a blender. Above her, eccentric insects and bizarre birds flew through the air in a vortex. They screeched and buzzed in all different directions.

But one sound caught Viv's attention among all the rest.

It was her mom's voice.

In the water on the far side of the arena, Director Harlow and Dr. Frank still wrestled over the plasma pistols. Shots rang out from Dr. Frank's weapon and fired in random directions.

Viv watched as one of the blasts rocketed off through the water and hit a giant salamander in the tail. Amazingly, the creature's tail grew back instantaneously.

"Mom!" Viv shouted. "Be careful!"

But her voice didn't carry far. The whole place was too loud.

Poor Dr. Frank.

She and her daughter were both having a particularly tough day.

I hope Charlotte hasn't been eaten by the Mothman yet.

Viv wanted to help, but she didn't know where to begin.

A splash of water sprayed her from below. It was Ray, in his gigantic form, surfacing from the pool like a clumsy whale.

Viv watched as he wrapped his enormous arms around the Loch Ness Monster's body. They wrestled for a moment, rocking tsunami-like waves throughout the water before Ray landed a left hook against Nessie's cheek. Its long neck recoiled from the blow.

"Take that!" Ray bellowed. "Did I forget to mention that I can get bigger, too?"

His voice had dropped at least ten octaves. It rattled her podium like a booming earthquake.

Well, at least Ray looks like he has things under control.

A whiz of green sailed through the air by Viv's head.

No way . . . It can't be. Meekee?

The little alien zoomed around the room in a levitating glide. His entire body was encapsulated in a glowing green light, a color that Viv knew all too well. The eerily familiar shade could only mean one thing.

Meekee has powers?!

Viv could hardly believe what she was seeing. She rubbed at her eyes with the back of her hands, hoping it wasn't some kind of hallucination.

I can't believe I never considered this before! It never crossed my mind that Meekee could have powers like mine!

Even though he was from the Roswellians' planet, knowing that there was at least one other alien with her powers on this planet gave Viv a sense of comfort.

But he wasn't alone up there. Circling him was his sworn mortal enemy: FuRo. Once again, Joanna's robot had taken the shape of a falcon. They clashed in the air like two fighter pilots, insistent on the other's destruction.

Viv remembered how brutal the robot's diving attacks had been yesterday.

I hope Meekee's better at controlling his powers than I am!

"Meekee! Be careful!" Viv shouted.

As the aerial dogfight took another spin around the arena, Viv's eyes settled on two shapes perched high above the waterline between a set of auditorium seats.

Elijah!

As happy as Viv was to see that he was alive, his current situation didn't look particularly great, either.

Looming above him, the monstrous white Yeti heaved her arms up in his direction. Over the raucous clatter of the arena, Viv could barely make out what they were saying.

"Roger!" Elijah shouted. "Please! Don't do this! I don't want to fight you!"

"Sorry!" The Yeti swung her fists toward him again. The beast's eyes glowed red under the Chupacabra's influence. "It's not me, eh? I promise!"

Elijah dodged another blow from her huge paws as they smashed into a set of chairs. He clambered up the rows of seats, trying to escape.

Why isn't he using his flight suit?

Before she could shout out to him, a set of fingers gripped the edge of the other podium opposite Viv's.

It was Joanna. Her hair, usually so perfectly straight, was wet and matted. She pulled herself up onto her belly and rolled onto her back, flopping over onto the platform like an exhausted seal.

Even the sight of her filled Viv with rage.

"Joanna!" Viv shouted over the din of the room. The anger in her voice was impossible to hide. "Why? Why did you do this?!"

Joanna didn't respond. After a few moments, she rose to her feet into a wobbly stance and looked around the arena with the same bewildered look Viv felt in her own eyes.

The tears started to sting Viv's cheeks as she couldn't contain the emotions brewing inside her.

"You tried to frame Charlotte!" Viv continued. "You tried to frame my best friend!"

Joanna turned, and her eyes slowly settled onto Viv's. Her lip quivered as she spoke.

Is she . . . crying?

"I am sorry about Charlotte," Joanna said. "It was the only way I could think of helping these poor creatures."

"Helping them?" Viv said. "Look around us. Does it look like you're helping them?"

The pandemonium happening around them was inescapable, and the water levels in the pool were still rising. Joanna took a few long blinks, looking even more unsteady than before.

"I still don't understand why you would handle things this way," Viv said. "Is this really how you imagined the great escape would go?"

"I couldn't live with myself if any of those creatures were forced to stay locked up in the Forbidden Zone even one more night!"

"So what?" Viv said. "You decided to send FuRo in here looking like Charlotte?"

"It was the only way," Joanna said.

"But these creatures . . . They're dangerous, Joanna!"

"They're misunderstood!" Joanna shouted back, her voice breaking on the last word.

Viv softened her stance a bit, lowering her arm cannon.

Her heart's in the right place. She really thought she was defending these creatures.

"You should understand better than anyone," Joanna said.

What? What does she mean?

"I heard what you did last week," she said. "Helping those aliens escape from their prison cells?"

Viv's mouth fell open. She snapped her jaw shut, trying not to let Joanna see her caught off guard.

She thinks I helped the Roswellians escape? Whoever told her that story got the whole thing completely wrong.

"You think I purposefully released them?" Viv asked.

"I heard you were on the ship with them when they escaped back to their home planet."

"I tried to stop them from escaping," Viv said.

"So you admit they were being held here against their will?"

"It wasn't like that at all. They basically kidnapped *me*. They tried to take me with them!"

Joanna's face curled into a grimace.

"Why would they do that?" she said. "Why would they wanna take you with them?"

Viv wished she could bite her tongue and take it back. She didn't know how to respond.

Because I have alien DNA? Because I'm a total freak of nature who should probably be in the Forbidden Zone, too?

"Listen. The truth is, I don't understand everything that goes on here," Viv said. "But there must be a reason they're holding all these cryptids here. Take the Chupacabra, for example!"

She pointed toward the ceiling at the beast clinging to the titanium rafters. Its eyes still flamed with scarlet fury.

"Look at what that thing has done to this base alone," Viv said. "Imagine if they released it back into the wild. All the pain and problems it would cause. Not just for the people but for the entire planet!"

Again, she got no response. Joanna stood as still as a statue, her eyes not knowing where to look.

I need to try a different approach.

"Joanna, I think your heart was in the right place, but I'm not sure you thought this through," Viv said. "And no matter what your intentions are, framing Charlotte and deceiving everyone is still wrong."

Joanna finally moved, folding her arms across her chest and holding her own elbows, almost as if she was trying to disappear into the podium. She finally cleared her throat and eked out a quiet reply.

"I never meant to cause all this trouble. I just wanted to help them."

"I understand," Viv replied. "And I promise you—if we get out of this alive, we will talk to my mom and everyone here at Area 51 to make absolute certain these creatures are happy and being treated well, and which ones, if any, can be let free. We'll do it the right way . . . together. Sound good?"

Joanna fought back tears and nodded in agreement.

"Now," Viv added. "Help me stop this. Before anybody else gets hurt!"

Joanna took one more look around the arena. Viv could see the resignation on her face.

"Okay," she said. "You're right."

Viv felt the relief wash over her.

Thank goodness. I don't think we could do this without her.

Suddenly, the Chupacabra let out a bloodcurdling snarl. It dropped down from the ceiling and landed on the podium, slamming behind Joanna with a bang.

"Joanna!" Viv called out. "Watch out!"

But she was too late.

The Chupacabra laid a paw on each of Joanna's shoulders and spun her around with a yank. Both of the beast's eyes shined with a red blaze, attempting to hypnotize Joanna from point-blank range.

The Chupacabra's tongue flicked out of its mouth and licked its teeth. Viv could see flecks of saliva melting into the steel podium below.

It's gonna bite her!

Viv aimed her arm cannon and pulled down on the trigger.

"Joanna, watch out!" she shouted.

The blast left the barrel and flew toward them. The Chupacabra leapt off the podium just before the blast struck, skittering back up to the ceiling.

"Joanna?" Viv said. "Are you okay?"

She turned back toward Viv. Her eyes burned like two torches, overtaken by the creature's evil power.

No. Not her, too.

"FuRo, attack!" Joanna shouted out.

The robot, who was still fighting in the air, left Meekee in the blink of an eye and dove toward Viv. Joanna clapped her hands over her mouth, trying to fight the commands the Chupacabra was forcing out of her. But it was no use.

FuRo descended toward Viv's podium at lightning speed.

"Joanna, stop!" Viv said. "I don't wanna hurt you!"

"FuRo! Dive!" Joanna shouted again. Then, with a grimace, she choked out, "I'm sorry, Viv! I don't know what's happening! I'm not in control!"

FuRo swooped by Viv's waist and slammed into her hip. The robot's sharp beak made contact with the metal on her combat suit, sending sparks flying into the air.

Viv was automatically transported back to their previous battle in the arena. The pain and frustration swelled back in a flash, and she could feel her anger building.

No. Not now.

Viv felt the heat build up behind her eyes.

I can't lose control here.

Between fighting off FuRo's diving strikes and seeing her friends and family around her facing such peril, Viv heart rate reached a fever pitch.

I can't let these powers out. Not now.

Not in front of Joanna.

In front of Ray.

Dr. Frank.

Elijah.

Even my own mom.

"FuRo, attack again!" Joanna called out against her own will. From the looks of it, the Chupacabra's powers had sunken into her mind ever further, like a poison. There was no hint of brown in Joanna's eyes anymore. Just menacing red.

But what choice do I have?

Between each respite from FuRo's barrage, Viv looked down at the mayhem still unfolding around her.

Ray's circumstances had changed for the worse. The Loch Ness Monster had changed tactics, now whipping its tail back and forth in Ray's face, dousing his eyes with the murky water.

Her mom and Dr. Frank had a new common enemy as they both struggled to stay afloat in the rising tides.

Even the Yeti had run out of chairs to break, and now Elijah was darting across piles of splintered wood to dodge each strike from the monster's forearms.

Everyone she knew and loved was desperate to stay alive. Viv needed to do something to protect them. *Anything.*

It's now or never. I have to do this.

Viv cleared her mind and let the anger overtake her.

Suddenly, her Roswellian powers erupted out of her like a bomb.

She bathed the entire arena in a massive force field of green light. Everyone and everything—cryptid, robot, and human—in the arena was suspended in midair, floating through the room as a calm fell over the stadium.

The force emanating out from Viv had launched the Chupacabra off the podium and into the ceiling with a thud. The creature was knocked unconscious on contact.

Like a wave, one by one, the hypnotizing red light in each of the creatures' eyes flickered out. The Chupacabra's telepathic control was broken.

The impact from Viv's wall of light had also sent Joanna tumbling off the platform. As she hovered above the water, she blinked away the cherry color that had permeated her irises.

The atoms of the water even seemed to slow down.

For the first time since Viv had been in bed that morning, everything was completely silent. A calm settled over the entire arena, and all her loved ones were finally free and out of danger.

With one last breath, Viv closed her eyes and collapsed to the podium, exhausted.

CHAPTER
TWENTY-FOUR

The light of the Nevada sun poured in through the window, coaxing Viv's eyes to flutter open. She bolted upright in a panic, though she quickly realized she was tucked under the sheets of a soft bed.

"Oh, thank goodness."

Director Harlow wrapped her daughter in her arms and held Viv's head close to her chest.

Mom?

Peering over her mom's shoulder, Viv recognized the place as the Area 51 infirmary. It was the same place where she had her broken arm treated just a week ago.

Behind Director Harlow, a group of other people hovered around her bed. Along with a bunch of nurses, two friendly faces smiled back at her—Ray and Elijah.

"Viv!"

The word practically fell out of Elijah's mouth. He rushed to her bedside.

"What happened?" Viv said. "What's going on?"

Viv tried to pull away from her mom's hug. Her head throbbed at the motion, and she could already feel dizziness trying to take hold. Her mom shushed her and rubbed the hair on the back of her head.

"Lie back, sweetheart," she instructed. "Take it slow."

"You gave your mom here quite a scare," one of the nurses said, adjusting the pulse monitor on Viv's wrist.

"I was really, um, worried about you, too, Viv," Elijah said.

Is he blushing?

He is! He's blushing!

Viv's face began to flush, too.

"You passed out on the podium, Viv," Director Harlow said. "You hit your head, but you're going to be okay."

"What happened?" Viv said with a squint, her eyes still adjusting to the harsh, bright daylight. "Back in the arena? All those creatures?"

"It was miraculous," Director Harlow said. "FuRo released a green cloud of calming pheromones. I didn't even know that little robot was capable of such a thing, but apparently Joanna had programmed that response in case of emergency."

Pheromones? What is she talking about?

"Joanna said that?" Viv said.

"Yes," her mother said with a nod. "We're hoping that we can harness that technology into making the Forbidden Zone safer in the future."

Wait, why would Joanna lie about FuRo when she knew the green light was coming from my eyes?

Is she trying to keep my secret? Trying to protect me?

"Where's Joanna now?" Viv asked.

"We're holding her in a secure room, for the moment. Unfortunately, what she did was wrong, and we've got to unravel a lot of it first. Suffice it to say, her time at Area 51 is over."

"But she was only trying to help the cryptids," Viv said. "She had good intentions at heart!"

"I understand that now," Director Harlow said. "But the best way to deal with problems is to talk them out. Not to take unilateral action."

"Mom, I promised Joanna we would review every creature in the Forbidden Zone, make sure they are happy and healthy, and release them if they're not needed here. Can you and I still talk about that?"

Her mom took Viv's hand in hers.

"Absolutely, sweetie. What kind of mom would I be if I said communication is key and then refused to talk to my own daughter?"

Viv breathed out a sigh of relief.

"I must admit," Director Harlow continued, "when Joanna made the mistakes she did, I thought that perhaps I was wrong bringing children into this facility. But then the four of you kids, yet again, completely saved all of our butts. Well done, team."

Elijah and Ray high-fived each other so hard that Ray

couldn't help but shake out his hand afterward.

"And thankfully," Director Harlow added, "the rest of the Extra-Normal Affairs team arrived shortly after you passed out. Once the Chupacabra became incapacitated, plucking all of the other cryptids out of FuRo's protective field and returning them to their enclosures was a piece of cake."

Viv shuddered at the thought of the vicious creature.

"I still don't get it," Viv said. "Why didn't the control button work on the Chupacabra? Back in the pavilion, I kept pressing it, but it wouldn't work."

Her mom breathed out a heavy sigh. "We should've realized it earlier. The nanobots that were originally injected into each of the subjects were suspended in the cryptids' blood. Only today did we find out that the Chupacabra had been circulating its own blood back into the goats we'd been feeding it, so the nanobots were completely gone."

"Totally gross!" Ray said.

"Agreed. But thankfully, we were able to recover all the creatures safely, and their enclosures are being repaired as we speak."

The door to the infirmary slid open. It was Mr. Mond. He entered with a mop, a bucket, and an Earth-shattering yawn.

"Geez, Director Harlow, you weren't kidding," Mr. Mond said. "You guys really have been busy!"

"Thanks for getting here so fast, Al," Director Harlow said.

"Not a problem, director. I finished clearing the water out of the main pavilion," he said.

What? But there must've been hundreds of thousands of gallons back there!

"You got rid of all that water with that mop?" Viv asked.

Mr. Mond let out a belly laugh.

"This thing? Heavens, no. When we updated the pipe system here a few years ago, we added a draining feature to every room just in case something like this ever happened. All I had to do was activate the spillover ducts from the janitor's closet, and the whole place dried up in an instant," Mr. Mond explained. "That, and the instant-drying mechanism."

Viv thought back to their soggy car ride home yesterday.

They do have an instant drying machine. Where was that thing earlier, huh?

Mr. Mond wrapped his arm around Ray and pulled him in close.

"I'm just happy to see that these two are A-okay," he said, giving Meekee a rub on the chin. "The second we get home, we're signing you up for swimming lessons, Ray."

Meekee perked up at the sound of the familiar word.

"Ray! Ray!" Meekee said. "Best friend!"

Mr. Mond dropped his mop onto the floor with a clatter. His jaw flew open.

"Meekee can talk?!"

Everyone else in the room let out a collective laugh. The chuckle made Viv's headache worse, but the relief it brought outweighed any of the physical discomfort. Nothing made her happier than seeing her friends and family were safe.

But there was still someone missing.

Oh no.

"Where's Charlotte?" Viv sat upright again, terrified that her friend might've been moth food.

"She's fine, she's fine. She's with her mom in the Forbidden Zone," Director Harlow said. She stood up from the edge of Viv's bed. "Would you like to go see them?"

Viv rubbed at her temples.

"I don't know if I'll be able to make it down all those stairs right now," Viv said. "Or back up, for that matter."

"Oh, that's all right," Director Harlow said. "We can take the elevator."

There's an elevator?!

Ray's face dropped. The words came out of his mouth exactly the way they sounded in Viv's head.

"Wait a second. You're telling me there's an elevator to the Forbidden Zone?"

"Of course," Director Harlow said. "You think we walk up and down all those stairs anytime we need to go in there?"

"That's what we had to do!" Ray said. "I think I got bunions on my feet!"

Director Harlow smiled. "Hate to say it, but that's what you get for sneaking in!"

✹ ✹ ✹ ✹ ✹

Sure enough, Viv's mom was right. There was an elevator tucked away that led down to the Forbidden Zone. And despite all the destruction and devastation, it worked just fine.

When the doors opened, Viv could hardly believe what she was seeing.

Agents, engineers, and construction equipment raced around the space. The tattered ceiling had been pieced back together. Not a single shard of glass remained on the floor. Through a massive team cleanup effort, led by Dr. Frank, the entire place looked almost brand-spanking-new again in a matter of hours.

"It's about time!" Charlotte's booming voice came echoing from around the bend.

Charlotte!

Viv sprinted toward the sound.

"Hey! Viv, slow down!" her mom called after her.

But nothing was going to stop her.

Charlotte leaned up against the plate of glass in front of the Mothman's chunk of woods. Viv threw her arms around her best friend's shoulders and crumpled into the embrace.

"Charlotte! You're okay! What happened? Did you run into the Mothman?"

"Oh, ya know," Charlotte said with a snort. "After a little while, we came to an understanding."

She flicked at the glass with her fingertips. Behind her, the black, winged shape of the Mothman swooped away at the sound, ducking back into the shadows with a fright.

Of course. Classic Charlotte.

Whatever happened while they were locked in together, the Mothman seemed more afraid of her than she seemed of it.

Viv smirked. "Honestly, I kinda feel bad for the Mothman."

"Hey!" Charlotte said. "That's the kind of greeting I get after you left me here?"

Viv's smile melted into a gasp. The words stung. It pained her to think that Charlotte was mad at Viv for abandoning her, leaving her locked here in the Forbidden Zone while the rest of them saved the day.

But then Charlotte's scowl disappeared, and she pulled Viv in for another tight hug.

"Get over here, ya doofus." Charlotte leaned in over Viv's shoulder and whispered in her ear. "Does anybody know? You know, about . . . *the stapler*?"

Viv scrunched her lips together tight. "No. No, I don't think so." She could tell Charlotte her suspicions about Joanna later.

"Your secret is safe with me, mate."

Viv felt Charlotte's arms squeeze even tighter.

✳ ✳ ✳ ✳ ✳

With the Forbidden Zone patched back up and the rest of the employees helping with the cleanup, the Harlows, the Monds, the Franks, and Elijah circled up outside the gates.

At this point, it was almost ten in the morning, and

everyone who had been at Area 51 all night was running on little to no sleep.

The Monds were the first to head home. Ray threw a minor tantrum over having to leave Meekee in his cat bed in the Extra-Normal Affairs office, but now that the little alien was displaying some of the Roswellians' powers, Dr. Frank wanted to keep him there for another twenty-four hours to make sure he was doing okay.

Elijah's dad arrived at the base a few minutes afterward. He and his son popped a new rotor into the flight suit and then drove home together, blasting the heat in the car the whole way home.

Charlotte's dad, Desmond, joined them at the base a few minutes later to collect his daughter. Dr. Frank elected to stay behind and help finish up all the repairs, not to mention the mountain of paperwork she needed to fill out regarding the incident. As her husband backed their car out of the parking lot, she waved them off with a rare smile, clearly relieved that both she and her daughter made it out unscathed.

The only people left standing outside in the Area 51 employee parking lot were Viv and her mom.

"Viv? Baby? How are you feeling?" Director Harlow said, placing her hand over her daughter's forehead.

"I feel a little better," Viv admitted. "But I think I'm ready to go home, too."

Viv took a few steps in the direction of their Humvee.

"Viv," her mom said. "Wait."

She stopped in her tracks. Director Harlow closed the distance between them and knelt to her daughter's eye level. Her mom inhaled deeply and said her next words carefully.

"I didn't want to say anything in front of your friends, but we need to talk about what happened back there," she said.

Viv felt her heart tie up in a knot.

No. Please no.

"What are you talking about?" she asked carefully.

"I was in the arena, Viv. I watched it happen with my own eyes," her mom said. "That green light . . . It was coming from *you.*"

Viv felt her knees begin to buckle. She wanted to faint. She must've still been in the infirmary bed, having a horrible nightmare.

Come on! Wake up, Viv!

Viv blinked away, but the reprieve never came.

"But it was FuRo!" Viv said. "Joanna said so herself!"

"Vivian." Her mom wrapped her hands around her daughter's. "No matter what it is, we'll figure this out together."

Viv had reached her breaking point. She was too exhausted for this. Every fiber in her body wanted to collapse again, to fold up into a ball and roll far, far away. She didn't want to cry, but she couldn't stop the tears from coming.

"It's okay," her mom said, pulling her in close. "It's okay. No matter what, I'm here for you, sweetie."

Viv sniffled and wiped the drops from her cheeks.

"Now I understand why Megdar realized I was pregnant." To her shock, Viv saw tears welling up in her mother's eyes. "I had no idea that something I foolishly did all those years ago would affect you in this way, and I am so sorry for that. But we'll figure this thing out together. We have all the resources of the base at our disposal."

"But then everyone will know, Mom! I'll be locked up!"

"Nonsense! I refused to let the nurses run any tests on you in the infirmary. This whole thing, all of it, can stay between you and me. No one is going to lock you up, Viv."

Viv pressed the heels of her palms into her eyes, hoping that all of this would go away.

Her mom pulled her in for another hug. "I love you, sweetheart. You're my daughter. I promise, no one is ever going to hurt you."

Viv heard the crack start to form in her mom's voice. She sounded legitimately worried, almost heartbroken for the fear Viv was experiencing.

"Why don't we go figure this out together?"

With one last deep breath, Viv nodded.

Her mom gave her a tender smile and reached out her hand. Viv linked their fingers and followed her mom back into Area 51.

CHAPTER
TWENTY-FIVE

The base had already started to fill up with the rest of the day's employees. Viv followed a few steps behind her mom, watching as her heels clicked across the freshly mopped titanium floors.

Director Harlow carried a tray of glass vials and waved at each person they passed, saying her hellos and good mornings to countless smiling faces.

Everyone walked around, completely clueless to the havoc that had gripped their place of work just a few short hours ago.

I can't believe how quickly and easily they covered this whole thing up. How often does stuff like this happen?

It's gonna be a loooong summer.

Viv stopped as they walked past the infirmary's open door.

"Isn't that where we're going?" Viv whispered.

"Oh no, darling," Cassandra whispered back. "We're headed to my private lab. It's way in the back, in sector ninety-eight. That way, we keep your secret in the family."

After a few minutes of gliding from corridor to corridor,

they approached the secure lab, and Viv was glad to see it was indeed quite out of the way.

As they entered through the reinforced steel doors, Viv suddenly felt a weighty hand land on her left shoulder.

"ARGH!!!!"

The touch startled a scream out of her.

But what scared her even more was the look on her mom's face when she looked up to see what was going on.

Director Harlow dropped the entire tray of vials in shock, and they shattered in a million pieces across the floor.

Viv watched her mom's face turn pale white. Her cheeks sucked in as if she was seeing a ghost.

"It can't be," Director Harlow whispered. ". . . *Ernest*?" The name slithered out of her mouth like a bad word.

With a start, Viv's mind boomeranged back to the desert; back to the Chupacabra launching Ernest Becker off the ridge to the dunes below. With everything that had happened in the last few hours, she'd almost forgotten about him.

Until now.

Viv gathered the courage to look down at the set of fingers resting on her shoulder.

"Vivian," he said. His voice sounded distant and full of static, as if he was speaking through a crackling transistor radio.

She felt the hair on the back of her neck stand up.

"It's me," he said.

Viv let out a few shallow breaths and spun around to face

him, but what was standing behind her chilled her to the bone.

He was only half there, phasing in and out of the room like a hologram whose battery was slowly dying. The edges of his body were full of grainy white noise, almost as if he was being projected into the room somehow.

But Viv had *definitely* felt his hand on her shoulder. He *was* here. Or at least, he had been here at some point and was now slowly fading out of existence.

She could see the anguish welling up on his face.

"There's . . . not . . ."

More static filled the room, and his voice grew weaker and more distant by the second.

"Much . . . time . . ."

His body faded farther away.

"Viv . . . it's me . . ."

As he disappeared entirely from the room, he cried out one final sentence.

"IT'S DAD."

Viv reached out to grab him, but the molecules that made up what was left of his body glittered and faded away through the air. It was like reaching out to grab smoke.

As quickly as he'd appeared, he had vanished.

Viv extended her hand out into the empty space . . .

But it was as if he had never even been there in the first place.

Could it be?

Could he be . . . my dad?

CRYPTOZOOLOGICAL SUBJECT NO. 61058

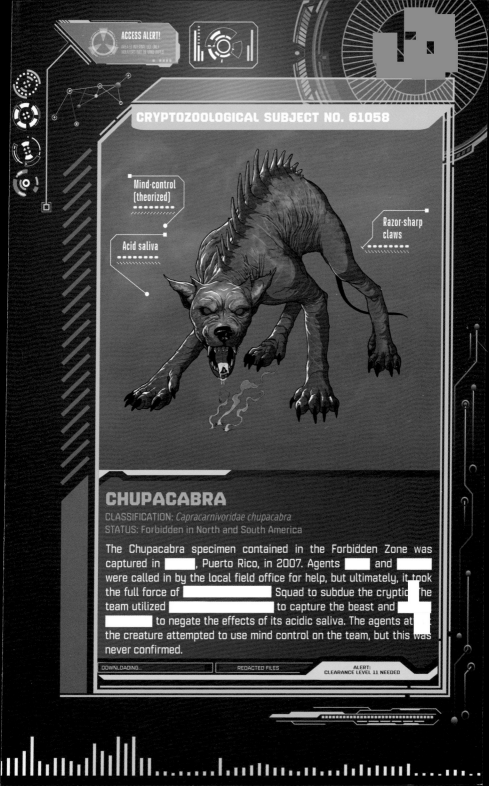

Mind-control
(theorized)

Razor-sharp
claws

Acid saliva

CHUPACABRA

CLASSIFICATION: *Capracarnivoridae chupacabra*
STATUS: Forbidden in North and South America

The Chupacabra specimen contained in the Forbidden Zone was captured in [REDACTED], Puerto Rico, in 2007. Agents [REDACTED] and [REDACTED] were called in by the local field office for help, but ultimately, it took the full force of [REDACTED] Squad to subdue the cryptid. The team utilized [REDACTED] to capture the beast and [REDACTED] to negate the effects of its acidic saliva. The agents at [REDACTED] the creature attempted to use mind control on the team, but this was never confirmed.

DOWNLOADING...   REDACTED FILES   ALERT:
                                                CLEARANCE LEVEL 11 NEEDED

THE FORBIDDEN ZONE

| Jackalopes | Jersey Devil | Mothman | Thunderbird | Yeti | Werewolf |

Hundreds of cryptids from the Western Hemisphere reside within the walls of Area 51's Forbidden Zone. Within each enclosure is a perfect copy of the natural biome where each creature originated, as well as porthole access to Area 51's larger terrarium. Each unique cryptid is forbidden from rejoining the outside world, for both their safety and ours.

DOWNLOADING...

CONFIDENTIAL

ALERT:
CLEARANCE LEVEL 10 NEEDED

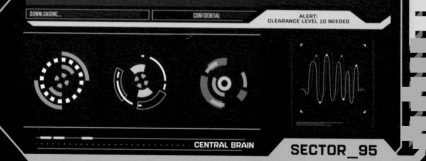